PUFFIN BOOKS

JUDi CURTiN

★ *The* Mystery Tour ★

Judi was born in London and grew up in Cork. She now lives in Limerick with her family. She has three children and a cat called Domino. Domino does not have any superpowers – as far as she knows. In her spare time, Judi likes to read, play Scrabble and grow tomatoes.

Books by Judi Curtin

FRIENDS FOREVER: THE TIME SPELL
FRIENDS FOREVER: DOUBLE TROUBLE
FRIENDS FOREVER: THE MYSTERY TOUR

www.judicurtin.com

The Mystery Tour

JUDI CURTIN

Illustrated by Sara Flavell

PUFFIN

PUFFIN BOOKS

Published by the Penguin Group
Penguin Books Ltd, 80 Strand, London WC2R 0RL, England
Penguin Group (USA) Inc., 375 Hudson Street, New York, New York 10014, USA
Penguin Group (Canada), 90 Eglinton Avenue East, Suite 700, Toronto, Ontario, Canada M4P 2Y3
(a division of Pearson Penguin Canada Inc.)
Penguin Ireland, 25 St Stephen's Green, Dublin 2, Ireland (a division of Penguin Books Ltd)
Penguin Group (Australia), 707 Collins Street, Melbourne, Victoria 3008, Australia
(a division of Pearson Australia Group Pty Ltd)
Penguin Books India Pvt Ltd, 11 Community Centre, Panchsheel Park, New Delhi – 110 017, India
Penguin Group (NZ), 67 Apollo Drive, Rosedale, Auckland 0632, New Zealand
(a division of Pearson New Zealand Ltd)
Penguin Books (South Africa) (Pty) Ltd, Block D, Rosebank Office Park, 181 Jan Smuts Avenue,
Parktown North, Gauteng 2193, South Africa

Penguin Books Ltd, Registered Offices: 80 Strand, London WC2R 0RL, England

puffinbooks.com

First published 2013
002

Text copyright © Judi Curtin, 2013
Illustrations by Sara Flavell © Puffin Books, 2013
All rights reserved

The moral right of the author and illustrator has been asserted

Set in 13/20 pt Baskerville MT Standard
Typeset by Palimpsest Book Production Ltd, Falkirk, Stirlingshire
Printed in Great Britain by Clays Ltd, St Ives plc

British Library Cataloguing in Publication Data
A CIP catalogue record for this book is available from the British Library

ISBN: 978–0–141–33512–4

www.greenpenguin.co.uk

Penguin Books is committed to a sustainable
future for our business, our readers and our planet.
This book is made from Forest Stewardship
Council™ certified paper.

ALWAYS LEARNING   **PEARSON**

For Dan, Brian, Ellen and Annie

1

'An A-plus in your history test is an amazing result,' said Mum as she hugged me tightly. 'Well done, darling.'

'I think you must have got your brains from my side of the family,' said Dad, and I knew he was really impressed.

My brother, Stephen, is usually the swot in our family, so even though the sudden attention was a bit embarrassing it was kind of nice too.

My sister, Amy, looked up from her magazine. 'Didn't you get an A in a history project recently too, Lauren?' she asked. 'Why the sudden interest in ancient stuff?'

Well, it's probably got something to do with the fact that recently our cat, Saturn, has been taking me back in time, and it's funny how history turns out to be a bit more interesting when you've actually lived it.

But I'd already decided that my family must never know about my time-travelling. (Amy would mock, Stephen would tell all his stupid friends, and Mum and Dad would ban any further trips on health-and-safety grounds.)

'Explain it to me,' said Amy. 'How do you manage to get two A's in a row?'

'It's called hard work, Amy,' I said. 'And until they start setting exams on beauty products and boy bands, you'll never know what an A-plus is.'

'Lauren!' said Mum and Dad together, and I knew that my special moment as their favourite child was over already.

It had been nice while it lasted.

Later on, my friend Tilly called over and we sat in my bedroom. 'So what's happening?' she asked.

I shrugged. 'Nothing. There's never anything to do around here.'

'We could go somewhere else then,' said Tilly.

'Like where? I haven't got any money for the cinema, and I'm bored of hanging around in the park.'

At first Tilly didn't answer, and when I looked up, I saw that she had a strange gleam in her eyes.

'I was thinking of somewhere a bit further away than the park or the cinema,' she said.

She was staring at Saturn, who was dozing peacefully on the end of my bed.

'You mean . . .?' I couldn't finish the sentence.

'Yes, that's exactly what I mean. We could go time-travelling.'

I felt a flutter of excitement, but it faded quickly. 'Scary things happen in the past,' I said. 'Think of everything that happened to me on the *Titanic*, and to both of us in Pompeii. Saturn never brings us to nice, peaceful places.'

'Yeah, but we survived, didn't we? We had amazing experiences, and we still got back here safely.'

'That's true . . . but –'

'And think of all the great friends we made in the past.' She was edging towards Saturn as she spoke. 'And now we know what to do. We know that if we press the stones on Saturn's collar, he'll take us back in time. It's simple.'

Saturn opened one eye and stared at her, almost like he understood.

I still wasn't convinced. 'The last two times, we went time-travelling by accident. It was kind of like fate. I'm not sure if I'm brave enough to deliberately go back in time. And, besides, we don't really know how the stones work. We could end up anywhere, and we might never manage to get back here again.'

Tilly grinned. 'It couldn't be all that complicated. And we're bright girls – we'll figure it out. Come on, Lauren, it'll be fun.'

Suddenly, I felt brave. 'OK,' I said. 'Let's go for it. Come here, Saturn, Tilly and I want to –'

Saturn started lazily walking across the bed, but

Tilly jumped up. 'Hang on a sec,' she said. 'Let's do this properly.'

'There's a proper way to time travel?' I said. 'Who knew?'

She giggled. 'Well, last time we really weren't prepared. We ended up like two dorks running around Pompeii in our school uniforms.'

'But we're not in our uniforms now.'

'I know, but still we need to make other plans. We need to bring stuff.'

'What kind of stuff?'

'Useful stuff.'

'But we don't know where we're going, so how can we decide what's going to be useful?'

'We'll have to guess, won't we?'

'OK,' I said. 'We'll bring my schoolbag anyway, because Saturn likes travelling in that.'

'And our phones, of course.'

'Mine's downstairs, but I'll get it in a minute. And you could run home and get your laptop.'

She sighed. 'I forgot to charge it this morning,

and what are the chances of ending up somewhere with electricity?'

She was right. 'OK, so forget the laptop. What could we bring instead?'

'We could bring today's newspaper.'

I shook my head. 'Mum won't let me touch it. Last time I looked, she was still doing the crossword.'

'We'll bring an old one then. If we go back thousands of years, a few days won't make a whole lot of difference.'

A few minutes later, Saturn was curled up on Tilly's lap, almost like he was resting for the journey ahead.

I'd emptied my schoolbooks on to the floor, and was folding up an old newspaper, getting ready to squash it into the bag.

'We'll need more than this,' said Tilly. 'We should bring some modern food. And maybe some colouring pencils – remember what a big hit they were in Pompeii, and maybe –'

She was interrupted by the sound of Amy screaming downstairs. 'You're always picking on me!'

'Oh no,' I said. 'Sounds like Amy and Mum are shaping up for one of their mega-rows.'

'It's just not fair!' came Amy's voice again, followed by the sound of the front door opening.

'Brace yourself, Tilly,' I said. 'When Amy's mad, she doesn't believe in closing doors gently. She always –'

Before I could finish, there came the sound of the front door slamming. It wasn't as bad as usual – I didn't hear glass breaking, and the house only shook a little bit. I was getting ready to breathe a big sigh of relief, but things started to happen very, very quickly . . .

The loud noise had made Saturn jump slightly in Tilly's arms, and as he did so his neck must have pressed against Tilly's arm, and Tilly's arm must have pushed on one of the green or blue stones on his collar. Then, before I could say a word, Saturn was shaking and Tilly's whole body was shimmering. Even though she was still sitting on my bed, I could see the pattern of the quilt cover through her legs. I only just had time to grab my schoolbag and throw myself on top of her when a familiar deafening noise began to rattle my brain and a bright white light washed over everything, and I knew for sure we were on our way through time again.

2

I opened my eyes slowly, and rubbed them hard. Something was very wrong. If my eyes were open, how come I couldn't see anything?

'Tilly?' I whispered. 'Are you there?'

Her voice was right next to me. 'Yes, I'm here, and I've got Saturn.'

'But we weren't ready,' I said. 'I hadn't packed the newspaper or anything. I haven't even got my phone with me.'

'Let's worry about your phone later,' said Tilly. 'Where are we? And why is it so dark?'

I looked around, but I was wasting my time. I'd never been in such a dark place before. I got to my feet, and was relieved to feel the solid mass of a wall behind me. Beside me, I could hear Tilly scrambling to her feet too, and I felt the tiniest bit better when she put her arm round me.

'Here,' she said. 'Take Saturn and put him into your schoolbag. If he runs off, we might never see him again.'

As soon as Saturn was settled, I began to feel my way along the wall, with Tilly following. 'I'll be happy when we get outside,' she said. 'This darkness is starting to freak me out.'

'But I think we *are* outside,' I said. 'I don't know why, but it smells and feels like we're in the open air.'

I heard her sniffing. 'Yes, you're right. But what kind of place doesn't have any lights at all?'

I was still feeling my way along the wall. 'Hey,' I said. 'There's something here on the wall. It's paper – like a poster or something. I wish we had a torch.'

'I'm an idiot,' said Tilly. 'We don't need to stumble around in the dark. My phone's got a great torch on it.'

A second later, Tilly was holding up her phone. After the darkness, the light was dazzling. We were on a narrow street, with darkened buildings all around. I could hear voices from inside one of the buildings, but there wasn't a single beam of light shining from any of the windows.

I rubbed my eyes and looked at the poster on the wall beside me. There was a picture of a woman carrying a basket of carrots, and underneath it said: *Carrots keep you healthy and help you to see in the blackout.*

'I mustn't have had enough carrots for tea last night,' said Tilly. 'I couldn't see a single thing before I turned on my phone.'

'We must be in the middle of some kind of power cut,' I said. 'But I wonder why there are no candles or oil lamps or anything.'

'Maybe it's not a power cut,' said Tilly. 'I think there was a blackout during the –'

Before she could finish, I heard footsteps and a man came racing round the corner. He was wearing a helmet with a big letter *W* on the front, and he did not look happy. 'Put that light out at once,' he said.

It didn't seem like a good time to argue, so Tilly quickly switched off her phone. By now the man was right next to us. He was carrying a torch, but there was some kind of tissue taped over the beam, so it gave only the tiniest glimmer of yellow that barely made any impact on the darkness.

'Why can't we have a light on?' asked Tilly.

'Don't you know there's a war on? If enemy planes see the lights, they'll want to drop their bombs on us.'

'War? Enemy planes? Bombs?' My voice was hoarse and squeaky.

'Don't you worry, lassie,' said the man. 'I and my fellow wardens will keep the streets dark, and no one will be dropping bombs on anyone. You'll be perfectly safe as long as I am here.'

'But it's dangerous walking around in the dark,' said Tilly. 'Anything could happen.'

The warden sighed. 'You're perfectly right. I've heard of three road accidents already tonight – the drivers just can't see each other with their headlights off. And last night a poor man walked straight into the river, and drowned before anyone could find him in the dark. If you ask me, we're all going to die in accidents, and Hitler won't have to drop a single bomb on us.'

'Hitler?' I squeaked.

'It's World War Two!' gasped Tilly.

'I didn't know this war had a name already,' said the warden. 'It was only declared yesterday, and I very much hope that it's going to be over soon. I fought in the Great War, and that was enough fighting to last me two lifetimes.'

'Er . . .what date is it?' I asked.

'The fourth of September . . . 1939.'

'And *where* exactly are we?'

Now the man sounded sympathetic. 'You poor things. Are you lost? Everything is confusing in the dark, isn't it? You're on Newbury Street. If you follow this wall to the end of the street, and then turn left you'll get on to Charles Square.'

That wasn't really the detail I needed. 'Er . . . I

meant what country and what city are we in?'

Now the man sounded puzzled. 'You really are lost, aren't you?'

'My friend gets a bit confused sometimes,' said Tilly helpfully. 'I think all this darkness has a funny effect on her brain.'

The man patted me on the head like I was an idiot. 'This is London,' he said, 'and if you don't know that, I'm not sure you should be wandering around on your own. Where are your parents?'

'At home,' I said, not even having to lie.

'And we'd better go home too, before they start to worry about us,' said Tilly.

'Do you know the way?' asked the warden.

'Sure,' said Tilly quickly. 'It's just down here beside Charles Square. Thanks for your help.' Then she pulled me by the arm, and we shuffled and walked and stumbled along until we had left the warden far behind.

Finally, we stopped and caught our breath. 'At least we can speak English here,' I said. 'All that sign language in Pompeii got a bit tiring in the end.'

'Yeah,' said Tilly sarcastically. 'Everything's perfect – except for the small detail of there being a war on.'

'But you heard the man – he's hoping it will all be over in a few days.'

'It's 1939! The war didn't end until 1945! Don't you know *any* history?'

'I got an A-plus in this week's test, remember,' I said. 'But I didn't answer the question on World War Two – I left out that whole chapter when I was studying.'

Tilly giggled. 'I'm telling our teacher that when we get back home.'

A sudden wave of anxiety washed over me. What kinds of things were we going to experience before we saw home, and Mrs Simms, again?

But it was a bit too soon for that kind of negative thinking, so I pushed the thought from my mind, and smiled bravely into the darkness.

'So what are we going to do here?' I asked. 'I don't fancy hanging around for six years, just so we can go to a big war-is-over party, do you?'

'Absolutely not. Anyway, it's the middle of the night. I'm cold and hungry and tired. Let's just wait till morning and we can make a plan then.'

So I hugged my schoolbag, and Saturn, tightly to me and we set off to look for somewhere to sleep.

 3

We spent a very long, very cold night huddled on some old sacks in a shed at the edge of a park. When we woke up and looked out the window, there was a grey dawn light and people were already walking through the park, looking like they had somewhere to go.

'Why is everyone carrying a cardboard box?' asked Tilly.

'Maybe it's the Queen's birthday,' I said, giggling. 'And everyone's bringing their presents to the palace.'

Tilly laughed too. 'Seriously, though,' she said. 'These people seem to be going to work. Don't they know there's a war on?'

'I suppose for some people, life kind of went on as normal,' I said, 'until the bombs started to fall.'

Tilly looked up anxiously at the grey sky. 'I don't suppose you know when the first bombing of London took place?'

I shook my head. 'No idea. I suppose that was in the history chapter I skipped. Didn't you read it either?'

Tilly looked embarrassed. 'Just the first few paragraphs – then it was time for this amazing TV programme that I just *had* to watch.'

I giggled, glad that my friend wasn't as perfect as she sometimes pretends to be. 'Do you think we'd hear the planes coming?' I asked.

Tilly looked really scared for a second, then she shook her head and sat up. 'There's nothing we can do about that right now. And if I don't get something to eat soon, I'm going to starve to death, and then it won't matter if a bomb falls on me.'

So we packed Saturn back into the schoolbag and set off to find some food.

*

We walked out of the park and along a wide busy road. Old-fashioned cars and buses drove past like everything was normal, like this was just any old day.

'I'd love a big plate full of pancakes,' said Tilly.

'Yeah, dripping with maple syrup and –'

Before I could finish, there was a loud wailing sound. We stopped walking and looked around. 'What's that noise?' I asked.

Tilly pretended to think. 'Well, it could be a special signal announcing that they're giving out free ice cream in Buckingham Palace today or –'

A woman nearby finished the sentence for her. 'It's an air raid,' she said.

All around us, people had stopped, but there was no sense of panic. A warden appeared and blew a whistle.

'Everyone take cover,' he said. 'There's an Underground station just round the corner.'

We followed a crowd until we came to the entrance to the station. I'd never been on the Underground before, but there wasn't much time to enjoy the experience. Everyone stayed calm, but a few people started to push and shove a bit as everyone tried to get down the steps as quickly as possible. We let ourselves be carried along until we found ourselves in a huge tunnel. There were white tiles all over the walls and the curved ceiling, and lots of ads for old-fashioned stuff. Tilly and I found ourselves a small space on a crowded platform and sat down on the floor. From outside, we could still hear the wailing of the air-raid alarm.

At first, everyone was quiet, and scared-looking, but after a few minutes, people began to chat quietly, and some even tried to make a joke of the situation.

A man passed around a bag of mints, and the woman beside us gave Tilly and me a ham sandwich to share.

'Omigod,' said Tilly as she generously fed her crusts to Saturn. 'I think you might just have saved my life.'

The woman looked surprised, but pleased.

I was still a bit scared. 'Do you think there are going to be bombs?' I said to Tilly.

An old man nearby answered for her. 'Probably not. The air-raid warning is just a precaution. Now, why don't we all sing a nice song to pass the time?'

Without any further encouragement, the woman beside us began to sing in a high, quavery voice, '*It's a long way to Tipperary . . .*'

'That's for sure,' said Tilly, and then we couldn't say any more as practically everyone on the platform joined in and sang so loud that we couldn't hear the wailing of the sirens any more. Soon, since I knew for sure that this was never going to show up on YouTube, I joined in too and sang at the top of my voice. The woman led the group in lots more songs, and Tilly and I hummed along to the ones we didn't know. It was like being at a very big, very weird party, and I was almost starting to enjoy myself, when a man near the station steps raised his hands and called out, 'Quiet please, everybody.'

The singing stopped, and I noticed that the sound of the sirens had changed to a single long note.

'It's the all-clear,' said the man on the steps. 'There was no raid. Must have been another false alarm.'

Everyone got to their feet and began to pick up their things and dust themselves down. I was really glad that the scare was over, but I had a funny feeling that some people were disappointed to be leaving. One old lady looked sad as she solemnly shook hands with all the people around her.

As Tilly and I made our way to the exit, a warden stopped us. 'Now young ladies,' he said. 'Where are your gas masks? Don't you know the rules about carrying them with you at all times?'

At last I understood why everyone else was carrying a cardboard box.

'Oh,' said Tilly, turning to me. 'Where exactly did we leave our gas masks, Lauren?'

I made a face at her. Losing a gas mask was probably a big crime. 'Er . . . we weren't at school the day they gave them out,' I said, 'so we haven't got any yet.'

The man sighed. 'Come along with me then,' he

said. 'If poison gas is dropped on the city, you will need to be protected.'

Poison gas didn't sound like a whole lot of fun, so we followed the warden out of the station and over to a nearby building. We waited outside until he returned with two cardboard boxes with string handles. 'Now,' he said. 'Here's one for each of you. I suppose your teachers did a gas-mask drill and showed you how to use them?'

I smiled vaguely. Gas-mask drills weren't exactly a big part of our school day.

'Oh yes,' said Tilly, smiling sweetly. 'We do drills twice a day, and three times on Thursdays.'

The man looked pleased. He patted us both on the head and went away.

Tilly opened her box and looked inside. 'Omigod,' she said. 'This looks like something out of a horror movie. Put it on quick, Lauren, and I'll take a picture.'

I took out the mask and was figuring out the straps and buckles when Tilly gasped.

'Oh no. My phone's not in my pocket. It must

have fallen out while we were sitting on the platform.'

We went back inside and searched for ages, but there was no sign of Tilly's phone.

'Someone must have picked it up,' I said. 'I wonder what they thought it was?'

'I don't care, really,' said Tilly. 'Dad's going to kill me when he finds out about this.'

I giggled. 'Look on the bright side. Your dad's not even born yet. You've got lots of time to make up a good excuse.'

Luckily, Tilly was able to see the funny side too. 'I'll worry about this in seventy years or so. For now, let's go back upstairs and make a plan for today.'

When we were back on the street, Saturn poked his head out of my schoolbag, almost like he had a right to be part of any decisions we made.

'So you want to stay here for a while, Tilly?' I asked.

'I don't really know. I've always wanted to visit London, but I'm not so sure I want to be here in the middle of a war. What if the next raid isn't a false alarm? What if bombs really start to fall?'

I shivered, even though it was a warm day. 'I sooo wouldn't want to be part of that. I was terrified when those sirens started going off. Even the all-clear siren sounds kind of creepy to me.'

'Totally. It seems a pity to go back home so soon, though. Who knows when we'll get to London, or to 1939, again? Why don't we hang around and explore for a few hours, and then when it starts to get dark, we can go back home, and we'll be there in time for tea.'

I giggled. 'Even if we stay here until the war is over, we'll still be home in time for tea.'

'Yeah, but you know what I mean.'

I nodded. 'Sure I do. Now let's go exploring.'

4

We walked around for a long time, and it was kind of fun looking at the old-fashioned cars and the old-fashioned clothes in the old-fashioned shop windows. Then we turned a corner and saw a long straggly line of children, being led by a few very frazzled-looking adults. Each child was carrying a small suitcase and a gas-mask box. Everyone had a label attached to them like they were pieces of luggage. A few of the older children were singing, but some of the younger ones were crying. Tilly and I stopped and watched as the line moved slowly past us. At the very end, quite a bit behind the others, was a girl who looked to be about our age. She was pale and skinny, with long, curly red hair. She was hobbling along with the aid of a single wooden crutch, half dragging her suitcase behind her. Her face creased with effort as she struggled to keep up. Then, just as she came near us, she dropped her gas mask.

'Oh fiddlesticks!' she exclaimed, shaking her head crossly. She bent to pick it up, just about managing not to drop her suitcase too.

A woman came back from the front of the line. 'Come along, Violet,' she said. 'You're being very selfish, delaying everyone like this.'

The poor girl didn't answer as she tried in vain to go even faster than before. The woman returned to the front of the line, and Tilly and I rushed over.

'Who is that awful woman?' asked Tilly as we fell into step beside the girl.

'That's Mrs Grimes, but I call her Mrs Grim. She's a teacher, and she's in charge. If I don't keep up, she's going to be very, very cross with me.'

'Here,' said Tilly. 'We'll help you with your stuff, if you like.'

The girl stopped walking and looked at her in surprise. 'Why would you help me?'

'Well, because . . . because you need help, and because we're here.'

The girl still looked a bit suspicious, but she dropped her case to the ground and watched as Tilly picked it up.

I took the girl's gas mask and walked along beside them. 'I'm Lauren,' I said. 'This is Tilly, and you're Violet, right?'

She nodded, but didn't answer.

Now that she wasn't burdened with the suitcase, Violet was able to move along quickly, and we soon caught up with the rest of the group.

'We'll stay with you until we get to where you're going,' said Tilly. 'And by the way, where *are* you going? This really doesn't look like a day-trip to the museum or to the local park.'

Violet looked at her like she was an idiot. 'We're being evacuated, of course. Don't you listen to the radio?'

'Evacuated where?'

Violet rolled her eyes. 'Being in London is dangerous. It's the first place that's likely to be bombed. So children are being taken to safety.'

'To where?' I asked.

Violet gave a big sigh, and I could see that she was tired and scared. 'I don't know, do I? I'll know when I get there, I suppose.'

'Wow,' said Tilly. 'That's so cool. It's like a magical mystery tour.'

I knew what she was thinking.

'Remember our plan about going home today, Lauren?' she whispered in my ear. 'How about we scrap that for a while? Being evacuated would be kind of fun, and we'd be safe from the bombs, and . . .'

She was right. 'OK, OK,' I whispered back. 'You've convinced me. Let's go and be evacuees for a while.'

We soon arrived at a railway station where all the children had stopped in the entrance hall. Mrs Grim came to where Tilly and I were standing next to Violet.

'So you got here after all, Violet,' she said. 'You surprise me. Now what on earth have you done with your suitcase and gas mask?'

'We have them,' said Tilly, stepping forward.

Mrs Grim looked at her like she was a piece of dirt stuck to her shoe. 'Who on earth are you? If I didn't know better, I'd swear that children are just appearing out of thin air.'

Tilly giggled. 'I'm Tilly, and this is Lauren. We're new.'

Mrs Grim did *not* look glad to see us. 'Where's your case then?' she asked Tilly.

'Er . . .'

I pointed at my schoolbag. 'I've got Tilly's stuff in here,' I said.

The woman looked at it doubtfully. 'Everything you need for the two of you is in that small bag?'

'Er . . . we like to travel light.'

Mrs Grim stepped even closer. She smelled of wet coats and old sweat. 'Did your parents read the government list of things evacuees need to bring?'

'Our parents are very responsible people,' said Tilly, not answering the question.

'Remind me what was on that list,' said Mrs Grim, 'or I might have to check that you've brought the proper things.'

She was reaching out for my bag. What if she looked inside and saw that the only thing it contained was a time-travelling cat with white fur and beautiful odd blue and green eyes? What were the chances of that being on the government list? Were Tilly and I in a whole lot of trouble?

Violet stepped forward. 'The three of us did our packing together,' she said, 'and we brought exactly what the list said.'

'Which is?' asked Mrs Grim, with mean, narrowed eyes.

Violet took a deep breath and spoke quickly. 'One gas mask, one skirt, one blouse, one cardigan, one vest, one petticoat, two pairs of knickers, two pairs of stockings, a towel, a facecloth, six handkerchiefs, wellington boots, a comb, a toothbrush, soap, a packed lunch and an overcoat.'

Mrs Grim looked sick. 'Why, that's exactly what the list said.'

'That's amazing,' I said. 'Did you learn the list off by heart?'

For the first time, Violet smiled. 'No. I just read it once. I've got a good memory, that's all.'

'I've got to hand it to you, Violet,' said Mrs Grim sourly, 'you're the cleverest cripple I've ever known.'

I gasped, but Violet didn't even flinch at the word 'cripple', or at the fact that Mrs Grim was surprised that a girl with a weak leg could be smart.

Now Mrs Grim turned to Tilly and me again. 'Where are your labels? Don't tell me you've eaten them.'

'Eaten them?' echoed Tilly.

'You wouldn't be the first,' said Mrs Grim. 'Anyway, I haven't time for discussion. Here are two spare labels. Fill them in yourselves and pin them on, and be ready when the train comes.'

Mrs Grim walked away, and Tilly giggled. 'I feel like writing *PLEASE LOOK AFTER THIS BEAR* on my label.'

32

Mrs Grim stopped and glared back at us, and Tilly shivered. 'Or maybe not,' she said.

So, using a pencil Mrs Grim had given us, Tilly and I wrote our names on the labels, and copied the other details from Violet's tag.

Half an hour later Tilly, Violet and I were sitting in a small compartment on a train. There was a loud whistle and the train started to move. 'Yay!' said Tilly. 'The magical mystery tour begins!'

 5

The train was warm and stuffy, and gradually
the other children in our compartment began
to fall asleep. After a while, only Tilly, Violet and I
were still awake.

I tapped Violet on the shoulder. 'Can you keep a
secret?' I whispered.

She nodded, and I began to open the zip of my
schoolbag. 'You see,' I said, 'Tilly and I didn't
exactly bring much of the stuff on that list.'

'Or actually *any* of the stuff on that list,' said Tilly,
smiling.

'Me neither,' said Violet. 'I don't own half of
those things anyway and, besides, I wanted to have
room for my maths books.'

'You brought maths books?' said Tilly with wide eyes, but before Violet could answer, I opened my schoolbag so that she could see inside. Right on cue, Saturn opened his eyes and gave a huge yawn.

Violet laughed happily. 'What a beautiful cat!' she said. 'He's absolutely perfect. Can I hold him?'

I looked around to make sure that everyone else was still asleep, and then I took Saturn out of the bag and put him on Violet's lap, where he curled up like he'd known her all his life.

She stroked and petted him, and then opened her own bag. 'Books and food,' she said. 'The essential things in life. That's all I've got in here. Anyone hungry?'

I suddenly realized that I was very, very hungry. Violet shared out sandwiches and biscuits, making sure that Saturn got some too. Then I put Saturn back into his bag and we all settled ourselves and slept for a long time.

When I woke up, the train was slowing down as it pulled into a station. It looked like we were in a tiny village in the middle of nowhere. 'Wake up,' I said to Tilly and Violet. 'We're here . . . wherever here is.'

Mrs Grim came along the corridor, flapping like a demented chicken. 'Come along, children. Pick up your bags and line up on the platform.'

We all stepped down from the train. Some of the smaller children started to cry again. 'Poor little mites,' said Violet. 'They don't understand what's going on. They probably thought their mothers would be waiting here for them.'

I picked up a tiny, sobbing little girl and tried to make her smile, but she just clung to me, like she never wanted to let go. I read her label. 'Lillian,' I said. 'What a sweet name for a sweet little girl.'

She smiled for a second, and put her thumb in her mouth, but as she snuggled in close to me, I could feel her little body shaking with deep sobs.

'How is this right?' asked Tilly. 'This poor little kid's much too small to be away from her family.'

'Maybe,' said Violet, 'but the government insists

that it's the right thing to do. London's too dangerous at the moment. We're safer here.'

Mrs Grim was back. 'Come along, children,' she said again. 'We're off to the village hall, where all your nice new families will be waiting. Now look sharp, I want to get back home to London this year, if possible.'

We left the station and walked along a narrow lane with huge hedges on either side. As we got to the end, the bigger children at the front began to jump up and down, laughing excitedly.

'I don't know what all the fuss is about,' said Mrs Grim impatiently. 'It's just the sea.'

Violet gripped her crutch tightly and pushed past us to the end of the lane, moving faster than I'd have thought possible. When we caught up with her, her eyes were shiny as if she was about to cry. 'The sea,' she sighed. 'I never in my whole life thought that I'd see the sea . . .'

At a shout from Mrs Grim, everyone reluctantly started to walk again, and soon we were at the village hall, which was already crowded with people.

Mrs Grim and the other teachers formed the evacuees into a straggly line, and then stood near the last child, ready to tick off names on clipboards.

'Ready,' called Mrs Grim, and the villagers began to walk up and down, looking carefully at us.

It was totally weird standing there, trying to be good enough to be chosen. 'This is even worse than picking teams for basketball,' I muttered.

'Much worse,' said Tilly. 'I don't believe this is happening. It's almost as bad as being sold as a slave in Pompeii.'

Lillian was still sobbing in my arms, and I surveyed the crowd, looking for someone who looked kind. Just then a little old lady came along. She was like a granny from a storybook with rosy cheeks and white hair.

'Excuse me,' I said, and the woman turned and smiled, showing little dimples on her round cheeks.

'This is Lillian,' I said, 'and she needs someone to take care of her.'

'Oh, you little darling,' said the old woman, opening out her arms. Lillian leapt into them, and snuggled against the old lady's fluffy cardigan.

'Thank you,' said the old lady to me, almost like I'd given her a present. The woman went over to Mrs Grim, who wrote the details on her clipboard, and then she walked from the hall, whispering to Lillian all the time.

Just then, I saw a huge red-faced farmer walking quickly towards us. He looked closely at Violet, but shook his head when he saw her crutch. 'I'm not taking a cripple,' he said roughly. 'You'd be good for nothing.'

I gasped.

'Hey,' said Tilly. 'You can't say stuff like that about a disabled person. Haven't you heard of discrimination laws?'

I doubted if discrimination laws had been passed yet, but suddenly I realized we had a more immediate problem. The farmer was looking very closely at Tilly. 'A feisty one,' he said, and then he turned to look at me. 'You and your friend are strong-looking too. You could be very useful on my farm.'

I sooo didn't want to go anywhere near this man's farm, but what could we do? It didn't look like the evacuees were being given any choice at all.

Just then a row broke out at the other side of the hall, where two women seemed to be fighting over a tall skinny boy. 'I need him,' said one woman. 'My Henry's signed up for the army, and I have no one to look after the garden.'

'That's all very well,' said the other woman. 'But I saw him first.'

While the red-faced man was distracted by the row, Violet whispered to Tilly and me, 'Start coughing . . . and scratching.' I didn't understand, but Violet quickly explained. 'He won't want you if he thinks you're sick or that you've got lice.'

The row seemed to be over, and the red-faced man turned his attention back to us. I put my hand over my mouth and began to cough. Then I used my other hand to scratch my head. Tilly went even further. Not bothering to cover her mouth, she coughed loudly in the man's face, and then she scratched her head like it was party central for lice.

He stepped backwards. 'You filthy little wretch,' he said. 'I wouldn't take you if you were the last child here.'

Tilly giggled, and gave another cough in his direction. 'Good, because I'd sooner sleep in the street than go to your stinky farm.'

He raised his hand like he wanted to hit her, but then he saw one of the teachers watching, and he moved along the line.

Soon, most of the evacuees had been selected, and the hall was nearly empty. I didn't particularly like the look of some of the adults I'd seen, but even so, it was kind of humiliating not to be picked at all. 'Will we be sent back to London, if no one picks us?' I asked.

'I don't know,' said Violet. 'Maybe you'll be sent back, but I have to stay here. I've only got my dad, and he signed up for the army this morning. He won't be home until the war is over, so I have nowhere else to go.'

'What's wrong with us anyway?' asked Tilly. 'Why isn't anyone picking us?'

'Well, we all know what's wrong with me,' said Violet. 'With you it's a bit more complicated. You should be popular, because, as that horrible farmer said, you're strong and healthy-looking.'

I realized that she was right. Most of the evacuees had been kind of pale and skinny, and looked like a decent meal and a few vitamin tablets wouldn't do them any harm. 'So why doesn't anyone want Tilly and me?' I asked.

Now Violet looked embarrassed.

'Just come right out and say it,' said Tilly. 'We can take it.'

Violet went so red that her face and her hair were almost the same colour. 'You both look sort of . . .'

'Sort of what?' I prompted her.

'Well, sort of peculiar. Your hair is different.'

I gazed around the room. Tilly and I were the only people who looked like our hair had been cut or washed properly any time recently.

But Violet wasn't finished. 'And your clothes.'

'What about our clothes?' said Tilly with a flash of anger. 'I only bought this top last week.'

Violet looked even more embarrassed. 'Your clothes are lovely and clean and everything,' she said. 'And they haven't been mended or darned, but they are a bit peculiar. I mean . . . you're wearing trousers.'

She said this like a girl wearing trousers was a big deal.

Luckily, Tilly saw the funny side of this. 'If we'd known, we'd have dressed differently, I promise you,' she said, laughing.

Violet looked pleased that Tilly wasn't cross any more. 'Shh,' she said. 'Someone else is coming, and she looks nice. Maybe she'll pick you.'

'Maybe she'll pick you,' said Tilly, but Violet just shook her head sadly and didn't answer.

The woman walking towards us looked about the same age as my mum. She was tiny and dressed all in black. She looked prim and serious, but she had kind eyes. When she spoke, her voice was posh and tinkly.

'My name is Mrs Chilcott, but you can call me Elsie, everyone does.'

She tapped Tilly and me lightly on the shoulder. 'Do you think you two girls could bear to come and live with me?'

'That sounds lovely,' said Tilly. 'Except . . .'

I finished for her. 'Except this is our old friend, Violet, and we'd really like to stay with her. Do you have room for three of us?'

Elsie shook her head sadly. 'I'm so very sorry,' she said. 'Even two is going to be a bit of a squash, but it would be impossibly dreary for a young girl to be stuck with just me. I'm taking two so you can be company for each other. A third girl would be lovely, but in my little cottage it would be impossible, I'm afraid.'

Tilly and I exchanged looks. What were we going to do now? If we turned Elsie down, what was going to happen to us? Would we end up with someone horrible? Or would we be sent back to

London and the blackout and the air raids?

Violet solved our problem for us. 'Just go,' she said. 'Don't worry about me. I'm tough. I can look after myself.'

Elsie patted her on the arm. 'I'm so sorry I can't take you, dear,' she said. 'But you can visit your friends any time you like.'

Violet smiled bravely and I could feel tears coming to my eyes. I knew we should help her, but I had no idea what to say or do.

Elsie was already walking away.

'This is all wrong,' said Tilly to Violet.

'We can't just leave you like this,' I added.

Now Violet looked cross. 'I don't need your pity,' she said. 'Go with Elsie and forget about me.'

Elsie had stopped walking and was waiting for us.

'We'll go,' I said, 'since we don't seem to have much choice in the matter. But we won't forget about you.'

'No way,' said Tilly. 'We'll come and find you tomorrow, and make sure you're OK.'

Violet smiled again. 'Thanks,' she said quietly.

45

I didn't know if it was right to hug Violet, so I just sort of waved, and she waved back.

'See you soon,' said Tilly.

'We promise,' I said, and then we followed Elsie to where Mrs Grim was still standing with the clipboard. By now the only evacuees left were Violet and a small dirty boy who had scabs all round his mouth. Mrs Grim ticked off our names, and Elsie walked to the door. I grabbed Tilly's arm, and held her back. There was something I needed to know.

'What happens to the people who aren't picked?' I asked Mrs Grim. 'Do they have to go back to London?'

Mrs Grim gave a huge sigh, like it was worse for her than for the two rejected children.

'Absolutely not. I'm in big trouble if they go back, and that's why it's so very annoying that no one wants them.'

'So what happens?' asked Tilly.

Mrs Grim shook her head crossly. 'I'll just have to find someone to take them, and that's very, very inconvenient for me. Now you people move along and let me get on with my job.'

So Tilly and I gave one last wave to Violet, and then we followed Elsie as she led the way to our new home.

 6

We walked along a narrow cobbled street, and I wondered desperately when would be a good time to announce that Elsie had taken on more than two evacuees – that there was also the small detail of a beautiful Turkish Angora cat.

'I hope you're going to like your new home,' said Elsie as we walked along. 'It's very small, but I make it as cosy as I can. And Tiddles will be so happy to meet you. I've told him to expect some guests.'

'Tiddles?' I asked.

'Oh, Tiddles is my cat. Didn't I mention him before? He's a real beauty.'

I figured this was as good an opportunity as I was

going to get. 'Actually, I have a cat too,' I said. 'His name is Saturn.'

'Oh, that *is* nice,' said Elsie. 'You're going to miss him, but Tiddles can keep you company until you get back to London to your own pet.'

'Er, Saturn isn't exactly in London,' I said. 'He's . . .'

Tilly helped me out. 'He's right here – in Lauren's schoolbag.'

Elsie stopped walking. 'Goodness gracious,' she said. 'That is a surprise. I didn't know evacuees were allowed to bring pets with them.'

I was fairly sure they weren't, but this didn't seem like a good time to point it out. 'Look,' I said, unzipping my bag. 'This is Saturn.'

I sincerely hoped that I could rely on Saturn's good looks to make everything OK, and I was right. Saturn popped his head out of the bag and Elsie gasped.

'Oh my Lord,' she said. 'He must be the most beautiful cat I've ever seen – except for Tiddles, of course. Look at those eyes – they're like jewels, and his coat is like gossamer, and . . .' By now she'd lifted Saturn from the bag, and was cuddling him. Saturn licked his lips, and almost smiled at me. 'You and Tiddles are going to be the best of friends,' said Elsie. 'I'm quite sure of it. Now come along, girls, we're nearly there.'

A few moments later we stopped outside a tiny house on what looked like the main street of the village.

'Oh, we're right in the middle of the action here,' said Tilly.

Elsie looked worried. 'Do you think it's going to be too noisy for you?' she asked.

I giggled as I looked along the empty street. 'I think it'll be fine,' I said. 'Remember we're from –'

'London,' said Tilly, quickly anticipating my mistake.

'I've been puzzling about that,' said Elsie. 'You don't sound like the other evacuees. If I didn't know better, I'd say you were Irish – but what would two Irish girls be doing in London in the middle of a war?'

'It's kind of complicated,' said Tilly.

'You see, our parents are Irish, but we've been living in London recently,' I said.

It wasn't exactly a lie. Tilly and I *had* spent the night before in the middle of London.

Elsie seemed satisfied with that vague explanation. She opened the gate, led us through the little garden and unlocked the front door.

'Tiddles!' she called as we walked inside. 'Mummy's home. Come and meet your new friends.'

While she was speaking, she put Saturn on the floor. As she did so, a huge ball of orange fur leapt from a nearby seat and flung itself towards us, hissing and spitting.

'Tiddles,' said Elsie calmly, 'be a good boy.'

Clearly Tiddles didn't want to be a good boy. He arched his back and hissed at Saturn like he'd happily eat him. Saturn stood his ground and gazed back at the orange monster. He was probably wondering if he should send Tiddles back to some time and place where cats were sacrificed and eaten.

Elsie picked up Tiddles and carried him to the door. 'You go for a nice walk to calm down and I'll get our new friends settled.'

She put Tiddles outside and then turned back to us. 'Your room is upstairs. It's easy to find, as it's the only one; my room is down here. You two girls go on upstairs and unpack.' She stopped and looked at my schoolbag. 'You don't have very much luggage, do you?'

'Not exactly,' I said. 'You see . . .'

We were in my bedroom, planning to go time-travelling, and my sister, Amy, slammed the door really loud, and so Saturn brought us back here before we were ready and . . .

'We left in kind of a hurry,' said Tilly.

'You poor dears,' said Elsie. 'Never mind. I'll lend you some nightgowns, and we'll fix you up with anything else you need tomorrow. For now, just unpack what you have and I'll make us some tea.'

Tilly and I made our way upstairs and let ourselves into the only room. It was tiny, with a sloping ceiling and a small window. There was one bed, covered with a beautiful white bedspread, and on a small table was a china bowl with flowers all round its edge.

'Lucky we're good friends,' said Tilly as she looked at the not-very-big bed.

'And lucky you don't have lice,' I replied.

'What are we going to do for clothes when these get dirty?' asked Tilly.

'You heard Elsie,' I replied. 'She said she's going to fix us up. Maybe she plans to lend us some of her clothes.'

'But she's only half our size.'

'Maybe we won't stay around long enough to need more clothes anyway,' I suggested.

'Yeah, you're probably right. It looks kind of quiet and boring around here, so a day or two would probably be enough, don't you think?'

'Yes. Let's just stay until we're sure that Violet's OK and then Saturn can take us back home. Deal?'

Tilly nodded. 'Deal. Now let's go down for tea. I'm starving.'

*

Elsie had set a table with a lace tablecloth and china cups and saucers. She made a big ceremony of pouring tea through a tea-strainer and serving us tiny sandwiches with slices of cucumber inside.

While we ate, I looked around. It was like a room from a museum, with ornaments on every surface. In the corner was a huge clock in a wooden case that reached almost to the ceiling.

'Do you like my grandfather clock?' asked Elsie when she saw me looking at it.

'It's lovely,' I said. 'Did it belong to your grandfather?'

Elsie laughed for a long time. 'Oh no,' she said when she could talk again. 'That's just what that type of clock is called.'

I felt totally stupid until Tilly squeezed my arm. 'I thought that too,' she whispered.

'My husband, Percy, bought that for me on our wedding day,' said Elsie with a faraway look in her eyes. 'The happiest day of my life.'

'Aw, that's so sweet,' said Tilly.

'But it was a bit frightening,' said Elsie. 'My father

disinherited me that day. He said Percy wasn't good enough for me and that if I married him, I'd never see a penny of our family's money. My father kept his word, but I never regretted my decision for a single moment.'

'That's like something out of a romantic movie,' I sighed.

Elsie still had the dreamy look on her face. 'Poor Percy saved for a long time to buy me that clock. He said it would keep time as we spent many happy hours and days together, but . . .' She stopped talking and looked really, really sad. I desperately wanted to change the subject, but that seemed kind of mean.

'But . . .' prompted Tilly bravely.

'Percy and I did have happy times, but not nearly enough of them. He died in the Great War in 1917. That's his picture, there on the mantelpiece.'

I looked where she was pointing and saw the picture of a young, serious-looking man in uniform. Next to it was a picture of another man, also in uniform.

'Who's that?' asked Tilly, who was clearly feeling daring.

Now Elsie's face lit up. 'That's Arthur, my only child,' she said. 'He's twenty-five. He joined up last month. But you'll see him when he comes home on leave. Now drink up before your tea gets cold.'

And so we ate and drank. The only sounds were the tinkling of our cups and saucers and the slow, steady tick of the grandfather clock.

Whenever I caught Elsie's eye she smiled at me, but I couldn't help feeling sorry for her. What would it be like to lose your husband in a war and then watch your only son put on a uniform and march off as well? Maybe my mum is right when she's always saying: you don't know how lucky you are.

When we'd washed the dishes and put them away in a tall glass cabinet, the three of us sat in the living room and looked at each other. With no TV or computer or MP3 player, or basically anything fun, I was sure that the evening was going to be totally boring. I was wondering how soon Tilly and I could go to bed so we could have a proper chat when Elsie started to talk. She grew up as part of a rich family in India and she told us really funny stories of the tricks she and her brothers and sisters used to play on the servants. Soon it was dark and the grandfather clock was chiming loudly, telling us that it was ten o'clock.

'Goodness gracious,' said Elsie. 'I must be boring you two girls to tears.'

Tilly and I shook our heads. 'No way,' I said. 'Your stories are totally amazing.'

'Oh, thank you, dear,' said Elsie, 'but even so, I think it's time for bed.'

She went to her bedroom and returned with two beautiful long white cotton nightgowns. She lit an oil lamp so we could see our way around, and then opened the door to let Tiddles in. He arrived in a fury of spitting and hissing, and this time Saturn jumped into Tilly's arms for safety.

I was wondering where the bathroom was when Elsie pointed out of the back door, and said, 'Privy's out there.' She handed me a small oil lamp.

Tilly followed me outside. 'At least there's no blackout in the countryside,' she said as we made our way down the short garden path. 'Imagine how creepy this would be without a light.'

I giggled nervously. 'This place could be disgusting. Maybe we'd be better off in the dark.'

But when I got to the toilet, I found it was probably as nice as an outside toilet could be. I waited for Tilly and then we raced back into the house.

'Can Saturn sleep in our room?' I asked.

'That's an excellent idea,' said Elsie. 'Otherwise he and Tiddles would be chatting all night and keeping us awake.'

I was more afraid that Tiddles would spend the night eating Saturn, but I said nothing. I just scooped Saturn into my arms and followed Tilly upstairs for our first night in our new home.

7

It seemed like only minutes later that I awoke to hear Elsie tapping on the bedroom door.

'Lauren, Tilly, wake up!' she called. 'You don't want to be late, do you?'

I shook off Tilly's arm, which was right across my face. She woke up too and we both sat up.

'Late for what?' I asked.

'For school, of course,' came Elsie's voice from the other side of the door. 'All evacuees are enrolled at the village school.'

Tilly and I looked at each other.

'School?' I whispered.

'School sooo wasn't in my plan,' wailed Tilly

quietly. 'It's Friday afternoon at home. We've just done a whole week of school.'

'I'm guessing it's not optional,' I said, as I climbed over her and out of bed. 'And it might be kind of fun.'

'And if all evacuees have to go, that means we'll meet Violet, and we'll be able to make sure she's OK.'

'Exactly. Now you didn't happen to see a shower around here last night, did you?'

Before Tilly could answer, Elsie tapped on the door again. 'Hurry up, girls. I've left your washing things here on the landing.'

I opened the door and found a jug of warm water, some soap, two flannels and two towels. I looked at them blankly, wondering what we were supposed to do next.

Elsie smiled. 'Maybe you have different ways in London,' she said. 'But down here, this is the way we wash.'

She brought the jug into the room, and poured the water into the big bowl on our table. 'I'm presuming you can work the rest out for yourselves,' she said as she handed us each a flannel and a towel.

'And when you're finished, pour the water back into the jug and bring it downstairs so I can fill it again for you tomorrow morning.'

Jumping into a steaming hot shower would have been a whole lot easier, but this really wasn't a time for complaining, so Tilly and I washed as best we could, flung on our clothes and went down for breakfast.

After huge bowls of porridge, we went outside and Elsie pointed the way to school. We thanked her, and started to walk, but she called us back. 'Aren't you forgetting something?'

We looked at her blankly. Was she now our surrogate mum? Were we meant to kiss her? Were we supposed to feed pigs or milk cows before school?

Elsie went back into the house and returned carrying two cardboard boxes. 'Your gas masks,' she said. 'You'll be in a lot of trouble without them. Now run along and I'll see you at lunchtime.'

We took the masks and set off again. When we came close, I recognized some of the evacuees from the train the day before.

'Look, there's Violet,' said Tilly. She was walking slowly along, doing her best to ignore a boy who was pointing at her and laughing.

Tilly and I went over, and when the boy saw us, he ran away.

'You're here,' said Tilly.

'And you're OK,' I said.

Suddenly I didn't care that it was 1939, and I gave Violet a big hug. She didn't seem to mind, and she hugged me back as best she could, while balancing awkwardly on her crutch.

'That kid was totally cruel,' I said when she finally pulled away.

Violet smiled a sad smile. 'He just doesn't know any better – and I'm used to that kind of thing.'

'So what happened yesterday?' asked Tilly. 'Did you find someone nice to stay with?'

The smile faded from Violet's face and she put her head down. Tilly put her arm round her. 'We're your friends, now,' she said. 'You can tell us.'

'It was awful,' said Violet in a whisper. 'Mrs Grim took me and Charlie, that boy you saw, and we went from door to door around the village, asking people to take us in. But as soon as the villagers looked at us, they all shook their heads. Some even slammed the door in our faces. And in the end, even though Charlie was filthy and kept saying very, very rude words, someone picked him before me. And then . . .'

'And then . . .?' I prompted.

She continued in an even quieter voice, 'And then Mrs Grim got very angry at me, and said it was all my fault for being a cripple. And when we got to the last house, she practically begged the man and woman to take me, and they did, but they didn't look very happy about it.'

'What are they like?' asked Tilly.

Violet shrugged. 'Not very nice. They said I couldn't share a room with their children, so I'd have to sleep on the floor in the kitchen. And I didn't like the sound of that, but I could see that I didn't have a choice.'

I hugged her again. 'Try to forget about it for now,' I said. 'We've got a whole day of school ahead – and it should be fun.'

School so wasn't fun.

First, we spent what felt like hours practising putting on and taking off our gas masks, which was really gross. Under the masks, our faces got all hot and sweaty, and the stink of rubber made me feel sick.

After that, we had lessons in reading and writing and maths. That would have been fine, except that there were about fifty kids aged from seven to fifteen, and the one teacher was supposed to teach us all at the same time, even though most of us didn't have any books or paper or pencils. Mostly the teacher just stood at the top of the class and shouted at anyone who dared to move or whisper.

I was really glad when the teacher announced that it was lunchtime. Tilly and I headed for the school gate. 'See you after lunch,' I said to Violet.

'But where are you going?' asked Violet.

'Back to Elsie's for lunch,' said Tilly. 'Aren't you going back to your family?'

'Family!' Violet almost spat out the word. 'My "family" told me not to come home until six.'

'But they gave you some food to keep you going, right?' I asked.

Violet shook her head. 'They said what they had was for *their* family, and since I come from London I was probably used to begging. They said I could use my crutch to get sympathy.'

I could feel tears rushing to my eyes. How could anyone be so cruel?

'Come with us,' said Tilly. 'Remember Elsie said you could visit whenever you like?'

Violet looked stubborn at first, but it didn't take long to persuade her to join us, and the three of us set off for Elsie's house.

When we got there we saw Saturn and Tiddles glaring at each other from opposite sides of the front garden.

'Oh good, they've made peace,' said Tilly.

I shook my head. 'No way. I bet they're just planning their next move. I'd say their fight is only just beginning.'

Inside, Elsie greeted Violet like an old friend, and the four of us sat down to huge plates of ham and eggs and salad.

After we had finished eating, Elsie gave Violet a package of sandwiches to take home with her. 'For later,' she said with a wink. 'Just in case you feel a bit peckish.'

Then the three of us set off for a fun afternoon of schooling.

After school, Tilly, Violet and I went exploring. We found a beautiful beach and we sat on the sand, enjoying the sunshine. I lay back and let the warm sand trickle through my fingers. The only sound was the lapping of the sea, and it was hard to imagine that this peaceful place could be part of a big war.

Violet gazed at the sea like it was the most beautiful thing she had ever seen. After a while she got unsteadily to her feet, leaving her crutch lying on the sand.

'Help me, please,' she said. 'I can't look at the water any more and not go in.'

'But you haven't got a swimsuit,' said Tilly.

Violet just laughed. Looking carefully over her shoulder to make sure no one else was around, she unbuttoned her dress and threw it to the ground. Then she stood there, shivering slightly in the breeze. In her petticoat she looked even thinner and paler than before, and her weak leg seemed wasted and useless. But her red hair looked amazing as it flew in the wind, and her green eyes sparkled as she flung her arms out by her side in joy.

Tilly and I rolled up our jeans and helped Violet to the water's edge. We stood there for a minute, letting our toes get used to the chilly water.

'I've only been swimming once before,' said Violet. 'My mother took me to a swimming pond in London. She thought it would be good for my leg.'

'She was probably right,' said Tilly. 'So why did you only go once?'

'My mother died shortly after that, and . . . well . . . I just didn't go any more.'

'My mum died too,' said Tilly, putting her arm round Violet.

For one second I felt left out, before I realized how stupid that was.

We edged slowly away from the shore. As soon as the water was up to her thighs, Violet flung herself backwards and allowed herself to float. Her petticoat billowed round her as she bobbed on the gentle ripples.

'Perfect,' she sighed. 'This has to be the most perfect feeling in the whole world.'

Violet stayed in the water until she was shivering and her fingers had gone as white as her petticoat. Then we helped her out of the water, and I lent her my hoodie to dry herself as much as possible. She put her dress back on and lay in the sunshine. Her teeth were chattering, but she was grinning madly. 'When I grow up, I'm going to live by the sea,' she said. 'And that's for certain.'

*

In bed that night, Tilly and I chatted for ages. 'So what do you think about this place and time?' she asked.

'Well, I know there's a war on, but it's not very exciting around here, is it?'

'You want to go back home?'

'I'm not sure. It's kind of nice here. Elsie is a pet, and I love Violet.'

'And being by the sea is fun.'

'And even though school's totally boring, at least we don't get homework.'

'Are we going to stay for a while then?' asked Tilly.

'I think so. If we go home now, it'll just be . . . well, home, and we'd be sorry we came back so quickly.'

'So a few more days?'

I nodded. 'A few more days.'

Then I blew out the oil lamp and we went to sleep.

 8

At school the next morning, Violet was standing
in a corner of the schoolyard. The boy from
the day before was there, pointing at her and calling
her names. Tilly ran towards the boy, waving her
arms in the air, and he ran away.

'Ha! A bully *and* a coward!' she called after him,
but he just laughed from a safe distance.

As we got closer to Violet, I noticed a big dark
bruise on the side of her face. 'Omigod,' gasped
Tilly. 'Did that boy hit you?'

Violet shook her head. 'No, he's just a stupid kid.
It was . . .' Then she stopped.

'It was who?' I asked.

But now Violet looked away. 'It wasn't anyone,'

she said. 'I stumbled and bumped into a table. It's all my own fault for being so clumsy. Cripples are always falling over.'

Tilly and I exchanged glances. I was fairly sure Violet was lying, but I had no idea what to do about it. 'You can tell us the truth,' I said.

'I just did,' said Violet.

I didn't believe her for a second, but she had a distant, unapproachable look on her face, and I knew she wasn't going to say any more. I put my arm round her. 'Come on,' I said. 'Let's go in.'

The first lesson was maths. I'm kind of good at maths, but Violet was totally amazing. She was able to work out all kinds of hard problems in her head without even seeming to think about them.

'How do you do that?' I asked when the teacher was busy with another pupil.

Violet shrugged. 'It's hard to explain. The numbers and letters just line themselves up in my brain, and then they make sense.'

'Cool,' said Tilly. 'Totally cool.'

*

At lunch, once again Violet didn't have any food with her, so we invited her back to Elsie's place with us.

'That's a horrible word you use, Violet,' I said as we walked there.

'What word?'

'Cripple.' I hated even saying it.

'Why?' asked Violet. 'It's what I am, after all.'

Tilly joined in. 'Where we come from, we'd never say that.'

'So what would you say?'

'Loads of different things,' said Tilly. 'Maybe "physically challenged" or "disabled" or something.'

Violet smiled. 'And if I used those words, would it make any difference? Would it strengthen my leg? Would it make me walk any better?'

'That's not the point,' I said. 'The point is that you'd feel better about yourself. You'd be more ambitious. You'd achieve more.'

'But what could *I* ever achieve? I'm just a cr–' Tilly and I glared at her and she corrected herself. 'I mean, I'm . . . disabled.'

We all laughed. 'That's better,' I said. 'Now come on. I'm starving.'

'Goodness gracious,' said Elsie when she saw Violet. 'What happened to your face?'

Violet couldn't look at her. 'I bumped it on a table,' she said.

Elsie looked at Tilly and me. We both shook our heads. We didn't believe her either.

'Violet,' said Elsie. 'Would you be a dear and pop outside and see if you can find Tiddles? I think he's in the back garden somewhere.'

Violet went outside and Elsie closed the door firmly behind her.

'Tell me everything you know,' she said.

So Tilly and I told her how Violet had to sleep on the floor, and how the people she was staying with wouldn't give her food, and how mean they were. We both suspected that one of Violet's 'family' had hit her and bruised her face.

Elsie took her hat and coat from the coat stand. 'Lunch is on the table,' she said. 'You know how to

make tea. I'll be back in two shakes of a duck's tail.'
And with a click-clack of her shiny black shoes, she
was gone.

Violet, Tilly and I were still drinking our tea
when Elsie came back. She put a suitcase on the
floor beside the table. 'That's all settled,' she said to
Violet. 'I took the liberty of packing your things for
you. You won't be going back *there* any more.'

For a second, Violet smiled, but her smile faded
quickly. 'But I have to go back. I have nowhere else
to go.'

Elsie patted her on the shoulder. 'You'll be staying
in my Arthur's room from now on.'

'But –' began Violet.

'There will be no further discussion on the matter,'
said Elsie. 'I had planned to keep Arthur's room free,
for when he comes home on leave, but now I see that
was very selfish of me. Arthur would just die if he
thought his room was empty, while you were living
with those evil, evil people. So the matter is settled.
Now is there a drop of tea in the pot for me?'

*

I felt really happy as we walked back to school after lunch. Violet had a nice new home and the three of us could have a fun few days together before Tilly and I went back to our real lives. Then we went round a corner, and everything changed.

'Uh-oh,' said Tilly, understating things a bit.

The bully was back, but now he had gathered what looked like a small army. The road was completely blocked by a line of boys, some of whom were carrying big sticks.

We stopped walking. Tilly and I were taller and fitter than most of these kids. We could easily run away. But how could we leave Violet at the mercy of the little thugs?

'Save yourselves,' said Violet, as if she could read my mind.

'No chance,' I said.

'Let's pretend we're not scared,' said Tilly.

Easy for her to say. My mouth had gone dry and I could feel my knees shaking. A boy at the back of the group bent down and picked up a stone. He pulled back his arm, getting ready to throw.

I couldn't help taking the tiniest step backwards.

Then there was a roar from behind us, and a tall, strong-looking boy came leaping over a wall. He grabbed the ringleader by his collar and held him up high so that his feet were dangling limply above the dusty road. He shook him gently, and the boy started to cry. 'I didn't do nothing, George. It was just a bit of fun.'

Still holding the boy, George turned to the others. 'Bobby isn't so brave any more. Anyone else feel like taking me on?'

No one answered, but most of the boys dropped their sticks, and began to back away.

George roared again. 'Gather up those sticks and put them in the shed behind the school. They'll be handy for the classroom fire when the weather gets cold.'

The boys seemed glad to have something to do. They rushed to pick up the sticks and ran off towards the school.

George put the bully down. 'Say sorry to the nice girls.'

The boy was braver, now that his feet were on the ground again. 'But I . . .'

George reached for his collar and the boy backed away. 'I didn't do nothing, but I'm sorry anyway.'

George grinned. 'That's much better. Now if you ever do anything at all to bother these girls, you'll have to answer to me. Do you understand?'

The boy nodded. 'Yes, George. I'll be good. Honest, I will.'

The boy ran off, and Violet looked at George like he was her knight in shining armour. 'You saved us,' she sighed. 'How can we ever thank you?'

George's face went bright red. 'No need for thanks,' he muttered. 'Now come along, or we'll be late for school.'

'I didn't see you at school yesterday or this morning,' I said as we walked through the gate.

'I have to help on the farm,' he said, 'so I don't come to school very often.'

At those words Violet looked so sad that Tilly and I had to laugh. 'Love at first sight,' Tilly whispered to me.

When we got into the classroom, Tilly, Violet and I went to the back of the room where the bigger kids sat. 'Come and sit with us,' I said to George.

George went red again and shook his head.

'Come on,' said Tilly, pulling his arm. 'Violet wants you here, don't you, Violet?'

By now George looked so embarrassed, it embarrassed me to look at him. 'I can't,' he muttered.

A girl near us looked up. 'George isn't allowed to sit with us,' she said. 'He can't read. He's a dunce so he has to sit with the babies.'

George turned and walked with hunched shoulders towards the front of the class. There he sat on a chair that was much too small for him, surrounded by little kids who all laughed at him.

'Omigod,' I said to Tilly. 'How cruel is that?'

But then we couldn't say any more as the teacher came in and it was time for our gas-mask lesson.

9

When we got out of school that afternoon George was already walking away. Tilly and I ran after him. He stopped and looked at us, embarrassed again.

'You don't want to be seen with me,' he said. 'I'm too stupid for you. I'm fifteen and I can't even read.'

'That's not your fault,' said Tilly. 'If you can't get to school often, then how could you possibly learn to read?'

George thought about that for a minute and then shook his head. 'No. I'm just stupid. The teacher says so all the time.'

'Since the teacher is so horrible to you, why do

you come to school at all?' I asked, figuring that in 1939 there probably wasn't a law forcing fifteen-year-olds to go to school.

George shrugged. 'No one in my family can read, so if I don't come to school, how will that ever change?'

What he said made perfect sense, but secretly I wondered how anyone could learn if they were constantly being humiliated and told they were stupid.

'Oh,' I said, probably sounding a bit stupid myself.

'I'd better go,' said George. 'I need to help with the milking.'

And so he walked away, and Tilly, Violet and I set off for the beach.

Once again, Violet wanted to swim. 'Come in with me,' she pleaded. 'You don't know what you're missing.'

Tilly and I hesitated. The water did look lovely, but I didn't fancy swimming in my underwear.

Violet guessed why we were hesitating. 'You can go in in your petticoats,' she said.

Tilly giggled. 'I would, except mine's in the wash.'

'Mine too,' I said.

So once more we watched as Violet floated in the water.

'I do so wish I could swim,' she said twenty minutes later as she was getting dressed. 'Don't you two?'

'But we can,' I said without thinking. 'I'm just OK, but Tilly's an amazing swimmer. She's won heaps of medals for it.'

Now Violet turned to Tilly. 'Will you teach me? Please? Please?'

Poor Tilly. I knew she'd love to teach Violet to swim, but that could take weeks and weeks, and we didn't plan to stay around that long. 'I'll give you a lesson tomorrow, OK?' said Tilly, half answering the question.

Violet beamed at her like she'd just promised her the sun, the moon and the stars all wrapped up together with a big shiny ribbon.

*

As we walked home afterwards, Tilly was telling a funny story but I noticed that Violet's face had gone pink and that she wasn't listening to a word that Tilly was saying. I looked up and saw George coming towards us.

'Oh my,' said Violet. 'He's all fancy like a movie star.'

Fancy isn't the word I would have used. George's hair was slicked down and stuck to his head with some greasy stuff. He was wearing trousers that were too short and a suit jacket that was much too big. The jacket was all crumpled and looked like a very large, very hairy dog had been using it as a bed.

When he saw us, his face turned a pretty shade of pink, perfectly matching Violet's.

'Where are you going?' asked Tilly, trying not to laugh.

George looked serious. 'I'm going to the next village to sign up.'

'Sign up for what?' I asked, wondering for a minute if there was a fun run or something like that coming up.

George looked at me like I was an idiot. 'For the army of course.'

'The army?' I repeated stupidly.

'Yes,' said George. 'There's a war on, and I'm not helping my country by ploughing fields and milking cows.'

'Well, food production *is* important,' said Tilly. 'People have to eat.'

He gave her a sulky look. 'I want to fight. It's my duty.'

George seemed far too young and innocent to be a soldier. 'But you're only fifteen,' I said. 'Does the army take fifteen-year olds?'

'I'm tall for my age,' he said. 'I can easily pass for older.'

This was true, but it couldn't be as easy as that. My sister can't even get into a disco without proving how old she is, so surely you couldn't sign up to a possible death sentence just by looking a couple of years older than you are. 'Won't you need a birth certificate or something to prove your age?' I asked.

For the first time, George looked unsure of

himself. 'I don't know. I don't think so. Anyway, I have to go now, or I'll miss my bus. Goodbye, girls. See you when the war is over.' Then he marched off looking romantic and young and brave.

I looked at Violet, who had the beginnings of tears in her eyes. 'Are you very sad?' I asked gently.

She wiped her eyes and tried to smile. 'Of course not. George is doing his duty, so we should be proud of him. Our country needs all the soldiers it can get. Now let's go home, I'm starting to feel a bit cold.'

When we got to Elsie's place, Tiddles and Saturn were hissing at each other across the living room. Elsie was sitting between them, calmly telling them to behave themselves. She jumped up when she saw us. 'I have a surprise for you, girls,' she said. 'I've been to visit all my friends, and everyone has been very generous.'

As she spoke she emptied a big bag on to the kitchen table. I gazed in silence at a huge pile of clothes. 'Now, no fighting,' said Elsie. 'There's plenty for everyone.'

I tried to hide my giggles. I'd fight *not* to wear most of the stuff on the table. It was all ancient and weird-looking – but Violet was entranced. She picked things up, and gave happy little sighs. 'I've never seen anything so beautiful in my whole life,' she said as she held up a totally gross dress made of purple velvet.

'Well then, you take that one,' said Elsie. 'As long as Tilly and Lauren don't mind.'

'Oh no,' said Tilly and I together. 'We don't mind at all.'

'Such sweet girls,' said Elsie, smiling at us.

We let Violet choose whatever she wanted, and then Tilly and I took a few not-too-gross things to keep us going while we washed our own clothes. Then Elsie produced another bag.

'There's one more surprise for each of you,' she said, pulling out three ugly things.

I was wondering what they were when Violet gasped. 'Swimming costumes!' she said. 'We can wear those tomorrow when you're teaching me how to swim.'

I wondered how we could avoid sinking to the bottom of the ocean in the huge, heavy knitted things, but I didn't want to seem ungrateful. 'They're lovely,' I said weakly.

'Totally cool,' said Tilly.

And Violet seemed to be speechless.

Since it was a warm day Elsie suggested that we have our tea in the front garden where it was lovely and sunny. We helped her to lay out a rug and cushions and a perfect white tablecloth. She put sandwiches in a basket and served tea in her good china cups. It was really sweet – a bit like a picnic in an old-fashioned film. Every now and then I looked around, expecting to hear violin music playing softly in the background.

When we finished our picnic, Elsie carried the cups inside. The rest of us were gathering the other things when a figure walked past the front wall. He had his head down, like he didn't want to be seen, but I knew exactly who it was.

'George!' I said as I jumped up. 'You're back!'

Tilly, Violet and I ran out of the gate and over to him.

'What happened?' asked Violet. 'Did they let you come home to say goodbye to your mother and to pack?'

George shook his head, looking embarrassed. 'The recruiting officer was a friend of my uncle's. He laughed at me and told me to come back in a few years' time when I'm old enough to fight for my country.'

'That's probably for the best,' I said.

'But the war will be over long before then,' said George.

'Hmmm,' said Tilly darkly. 'I wouldn't bet on that.'

Before anyone could ask her what she meant, Elsie was calling us from inside. 'Come along, girls, and help me to tidy up.'

'See you at school tomorrow?' Violet asked George.

You'd think being at school would be more fun

than running around a battlefield dodging bombs and bullets, but George looked like school was the worst thing he could think of.

'Maybe,' he said, and then he walked away.

Later, we had another night of Elsie's storytelling, and that was the end of another totally wild day in 1939.

10

After school the next day, Violet, Tilly and I went to the beach again. Elsie had made us sandwiches, and we'd packed towels and our super-fashionable swimming costumes.

Once we were settled, Tilly held up the three costumes. 'I can't decide which one I want,' she said.

I knew what she meant. It was kind of hard to decide if any one was slightly less gross than the others. In the end we closed our eyes and took one each, and we wriggled under our towels until we were ready.

I felt like a total idiot standing on the beach in a swimming costume that looked like it had been hand-knitted by someone who was colour blind . . . and not very good at knitting. It wasn't any consolation seeing my two friends looking just as weird.

Tilly giggled. 'I sooo wish I had my phone, Lauren,' she said. 'I'd give anything to put a picture of you on Facebook.'

For the first time in my life, I was glad not to be within a hundred kilometres of the nearest mobile phone.

'Phone?' asked Violet in a puzzled voice.

'Oh, did I say phone? I meant camera,' said Tilly quickly.

'You've got a camera?' asked Violet, sounding even more puzzled than before.

'Oh, forget it,' laughed Tilly. 'I was just kidding. Here, Violet, lean on me, and I bet we're in the water before Lauren.'

We stayed in the water until we were nearly as blue as Tilly's swimming costume. By then, Violet could already swim a few strokes.

'It's so wonderful,' she said, as we got dressed. 'In

the water I feel strong, and free. When I swim, it doesn't matter that my leg is weak, and that I can't walk properly.'

'And, like your mum said, swimming will probably make your leg stronger too,' said Tilly.

'So you'll help me every day?' asked Violet with shining eyes. 'I want to keep learning until I can swim to that rock way over there.'

I looked where she was pointing and saw a rock that was maybe a hundred metres further along the shore. That would be a lot of swimming lessons, and a lot of time. Tilly and I weren't planning to be there for much longer and, even if we were, surely it was soon going to be too cold for swimming in the sea.

'Pretty please?' said Violet. 'It would mean so much to me.'

Tilly looked uncomfortable. 'We'll see,' she said.

That's what my mum says when she means no, so I couldn't blame Violet for looking disappointed, and no one said much as we packed up our things and set off for home.

On the way we met George. Tilly and I kept the conversation going, while George and Violet took shy glances at each other whenever they thought the other one wasn't looking. It was totally sweet and romantic . . . until George said he had to go and muck out the pig's shed. We were saying our goodbyes when suddenly Tilly called George back. 'Hey, George,' she said. 'I don't suppose you can swim, can you?'

He smiled. 'I can actually. I often go to the beach with my brothers.'

'That's brilliant news,' said Tilly.

'It is?' said Violet.

At first I didn't understand either, but then Tilly made herself perfectly clear. 'I've been teaching Violet to swim, but if Lauren and I have to go away, would you continue her lessons, George?'

Now he was so pleased he looked like he was going to explode. 'I would love to do that.'

Violet looked happy too, but then her smile faded. 'Are you going somewhere, Tilly? I know there haven't been any bombings yet, but that doesn't mean it's safe to go back to London.'

'Oh, you know,' said Tilly vaguely. 'I'm just saying that in case we have to leave suddenly, that's all. You've made so much progress at swimming, I wouldn't like it to be wasted.'

That half-explanation seemed to satisfy Violet, and the subject was closed.

Much later, Tilly and I said goodnight to Violet and Elsie and went up to our room. Tilly sat on the bed, with a determined look on her face. 'You think we should go back home, don't you?' I asked.

Tilly nodded. 'Yeah, I do. I think it's time for us to go.'

'I'm not so sure. We didn't achieve much here, did we?'

'What do you mean?'

'The last two times I time-travelled, I really felt like I made a difference. I think I saved Mary on the *Titanic*, and we know we saved Prima's family from the volcano in Pompeii.'

Tilly thought for a minute. 'Well, we did achieve

something while we were here. We helped to get Violet away from her evil first host family, and we arranged her swimming lessons with George.'

'I suppose so. Now that Violet's happy here with Elsie, she'll be fine without us, but . . .'

'But what?'

'But I still can't help feeling that something bigger, something more dramatic should have happened while we were here.'

Tilly grinned. 'Drama's not always good. And remember, at home it's still only Friday night. You can come to my place for pizza if you like, and tomorrow we can go time-travelling again. Maybe we could go to Ancient Egypt – I'd totally love to meet Cleopatra.'

I laughed. 'OK,' I said. 'You've convinced me. It's time to go home.'

We didn't have anything to pack, so were ready in seconds.

'What about Elsie?' I said. 'She's been really nice to us, and it would be kind of mean to just vanish.'

'I know – and I hate running out on Violet too,

but explaining is going to be very complicated. Why don't we just leave them each a note, saying we had to go back to London in a hurry?'

It didn't seem like a perfect solution, but I couldn't think of anything better.

'I suppose so,' I said.

'I'll write the notes, while you go get Saturn.'

'Sure,' I said. 'Is he still downstairs?'

Tilly shrugged. 'I think so. Last time I saw him, he was having a hissing match with Tiddles – and it looked like Tiddles was winning.'

'Poor Saturn, he's had a hard time here. I bet he'll be really glad to get home for a rest.'

I tiptoed downstairs, glad to see that Violet and Elsie had gone to bed. 'Saturn?' I whispered. 'Where are you?'

But there was no sign of him. I took the oil lamp and checked the front and back gardens, but he wasn't there either. Tilly came downstairs, wondering what was taking me so long, and the two of us sneaked out of the front garden. It was kind of weird walking through the dark, deserted streets, and I held on to Tilly's arm for comfort. We searched the whole village, calling Saturn's name as loudly as we dared. An hour later, we still hadn't found him, so we made our way back and up to our room.

'This is very, very scary,' I said. 'What if Saturn doesn't come back?'

'He *will* come back,' said Tilly. 'He's a cat, and cats often go wandering. When we wake up in the morning, I bet he'll be sitting on the front doorstep, waiting for his breakfast.'

'But what if he isn't?'

'He will be,' said Tilly firmly.

I knew she was trying to be positive, but she's been my friend forever, so I could tell that deep down she was very worried too.

We blew out the oil lamp, and settled down for what turned out to be a very long, restless night.

When I woke up the next morning, I was exhausted. I left Tilly sleeping, and raced downstairs and outside to the front garden. Tiddles was sunning himself on the wall, but there was no sign of

Saturn. I checked the back garden, and then returned to the front and checked the road outside the house. It was no use though – Saturn was nowhere to be seen. I started to panic. I probably looked like a total idiot wearing Elsie's long white nightgown as I raced up and down, shouting Saturn's name. I was making a fool of myself for nothing, though, as after twenty minutes of calling there wasn't a single trace of my precious pet cat.

It was Saturday, so Violet, Tilly and I spent most of the day searching. When George finished his farm work he joined us too, but none of it helped – it was as if Saturn had vanished from the face of the earth.

Elsie hugged me when I got home that evening. 'You poor little darling,' she said. 'I know exactly how you feel.'

I knew she was trying to be kind, but the truth was, she had *no* idea how I felt. It wasn't just that my pet was missing. There was also the small detail that, without him, Tilly and I could be trapped in the past forever.

In bed that night, I couldn't stop crying. 'This so isn't fun any more,' I sobbed. 'This is serious. We're trapped, and there's not a single thing we can do about it. Why didn't we stay at home where we were safe?'

Tilly hugged me. 'Let's not get too upset too soon,' she said.

'I bet it's all Tiddles's fault. Saturn was tired of being bullied, so he's decided to run away.'

'Saturn's only been gone for a day. Remember we lost him for weeks after we got back from Pompeii.'

'That was sooo different,' I said. 'At least we were in the right time and place when he vanished before. And the woman who found him got my mobile number from his collar and rang me. If someone finds him now, my phone number will make no sense at all to them. And even if it did, and they somehow magically managed to ring it, my phone's at home on the kitchen table, and I couldn't answer it anyway.'

'Try not to worry,' said Tilly, patting my back.

'How can I not worry? Saturn could be back in Pompeii hanging out with Prima, or he could be on the *Titanic*, or he could be in the future. He could be anywhere at all.'

I shuddered as the awful truth struck me. 'You know we might never, ever get out of here?'

Tilly nodded. 'I know. I wonder what will happen when the war is over. All the evacuees will go home, but we won't have a home to go to. Our parents aren't even born yet.'

'My friend Mary from the *Titanic* has been born. She's in New York at the moment.'

'Wow,' said Tilly. 'I'd love to go to New York.'

'Yeah, but even if we managed to get there, how would I explain that I'm still twelve, even though she's . . . forty or something? I'm still a kid, even though she's all grown-up and has kids of her own.'

'That's totally weird,' said Tilly.

'Maybe we could get a boat to Ireland and go to stay with our grandparents,' I said.

'Yeah, imagine the surprise they'd get.'

I had to laugh. 'Imagine how *you'd* feel if two weirdos in funny clothes showed up at your door, and one of them said she was your granddaughter.'

'Even though I didn't have any kids yet? That'd just be creepy.'

'Totally.'

'Hey,' she said suddenly. 'By the time the war is over we'll be nearly eighteen. We could move to London, and get jobs and move into a flat together. That would be kind of cool.'

'Yeah, but I miss my family. I don't want to have to wait decades to see them again. And besides, I like my real life and want to go back there. I've got a big hockey match next week.'

'And I've got a swimming gala.' She gave a small laugh. 'And if Saturn doesn't come back, I'll be in my eighties by the time that gala comes around. I don't think I'll be allowed to swim in the under-fourteens category any more.'

Then I thought of something else. 'Can we be born if we're still here?' I asked. 'I've thought of something totally gross. Maybe we could . . .'

I stopped talking, and I could feel my face going red.

'We could what?' asked Tilly.

I'd been planning to say – *maybe we could go to the hospital and watch our mothers giving birth to us.* But then I remembered that since Tilly had no memories of her mother, talking of seeing her giving birth was really weird and cruel.

So I just shrugged. 'Oh, nothing,' I said.

For once in her life, Tilly accepted this half-answer. 'I bet you any money Saturn's back in the morning,' she said. 'And we'll both feel totally stupid for even having this conversation. Now try to get some sleep. Tomorrow we'll be going home.'

 **11**

But we didn't go anywhere the next day, or the day after that. Day and days, and then weeks passed. Tilly and I went to school, and went to the beach and hung out with our new friends. But all day, every day, no matter what I was doing, I was watching out for Saturn, so that he could take us home.

One Thursday afternoon, Tilly, Violet, George and I all went to the beach for a swim as usual. 'The weather's getting colder,' said Tilly as we wrapped ourselves in our towels and pulled on our swimming costumes.

'That means extra work for me then,' said George.

'Why?' I asked. 'I thought there would be less work on a farm in cold weather.'

'Not always,' said George. 'If it gets cold, the grass stops growing so I have to carry out food for the livestock. And then there's my work for the Morgan family at The Willows.'

The Willows was a huge house at the end of a long driveway on the edge of the village.

'Wow,' I said. 'I never knew you worked there.'

'I've worked there for years,' he said. 'Since I was a boy.'

As far as I was concerned, he still *was* a boy, but I decided not to mention that.

'What do you do there?' asked Tilly.

'When the Morgans are away and the weather is cold, like now, I have to go up every day and light fires so the place doesn't get damp.'

'And are the Morgans away now?' I asked.

He nodded. 'They left a few days ago. They've gone to stay in Canada until the war is over.'

'I hope they're patient people,' muttered Tilly.

'I wouldn't care about a stupid war,' sighed

Violet. 'If I had a house like The Willows, I'd never, ever leave it.'

'If we don't get a move on, we'll never even leave this beach,' said Tilly. 'I'm freezing. I'm sorry, Violet, but this might have to be your last swimming lesson.'

'But I haven't swum to the rock yet,' said Violet.

Tilly grinned. 'That's why I mentioned it. You've been doing really well, and I think it's time to try.'

We helped Violet into the water. Tilly and George swam beside her, while I ran along the shore shouting encouragement. I'd noticed recently that Violet's leg seemed stronger, and she could walk further without getting tired, but on dry land she still looked a bit awkward. In the water, though, things were totally different – she was sleek and graceful, and I was fairly sure that, given enough time, she'd be as good a swimmer as Tilly was. Violet reached the rock easily and hung on to it, gasping and laughing. I swam out to them, and the three of us hugged for a long time, while George doggy-paddled nearby looking pleased and embarrassed. It was a very special moment.

When we got back home, we all rushed to tell Elsie the good news, but when she opened the door, she looked very serious.

'What is it?' I asked, terrified that she'd had bad news about Arthur.

'Come in and sit down, girls,' she said. 'We need to talk.'

The four of us sat round the kitchen table, and Elsie started what sounded like a rehearsed speech. 'You know that there have been no bombings in London, or indeed anywhere in England?'

We all nodded. Now that we lived in a war, I was learning to pay attention to the radio (or the wireless as Elsie called it).

'I read in the newspaper today that they are calling this a "phoney war",' continued Elsie.

At last I could see where this was heading.

'And since there doesn't seem to be any danger, lots of the evacuees are going home.'

I'd noticed that. Every day there seemed to be a few more empty desks in our classroom.

'So . . .' Elsie began, and then hesitated.

'You want us to leave,' said Tilly. 'We totally understand. It was nice of you to put up with us for so long.'

I gulped. Bombs or no bombs, I really didn't fancy going back to London – especially without Saturn. How would he ever find us in a city that size?

'No, that isn't it at all,' said Elsie. 'You could never imagine how much I love having you girls here. You make this house feel alive again. But tomorrow is a big day.'

'It is?' I asked.

'Yes,' said Elsie. 'It's the twenty-ninth of September – National Registration Day. Every householder has to fill in a form saying who lives with them.'

'Like a census,' I said.

'Exactly,' said Elsie. 'Except that, because of the war, this one is particularly important. The information gathered now will be used if rationing is brought in.'

Tilly made a face. 'I've heard about rationing.

Doesn't that mean no sweets and no oranges and no sugar – basically no nice stuff at all?'

'How come they never ration stuff like cabbage or broccoli?' I muttered.

Elsie smiled at us. 'Let's all hope and pray that it doesn't come to any kind of rationing. For now, though, if you are thinking of going home, this might be a good time, so that you will be registered in the right place. Just let me know what you want to do.'

We all looked at each other. I could see tears coming to Violet's eyes.

'I haven't got anywhere to go,' she said. 'My father's gone away with the army – I don't even know where he is.'

Elsie patted her arm. 'Then you'll stay right here with me, for as long as you like. Now what about you two girls? Your families must be missing you.'

Tilly and I looked at each other. 'I know they are missing us,' said Tilly. 'But I think they'd like us to stay here for a while – to make certain sure that we're going to be safe.'

Elsie clapped her hands together like a little girl. 'That is all just perfect,' she said. 'It's exactly what I was hoping for. I'll put all three of your names on the form, and we can live happily here together for as long as you want.'

I gulped. My happy-ever-after didn't involve being stuck in the past forever.

'Oh, and one more thing,' said Elsie. 'I've been to the post office and I got some stamps and envelopes for you to write to your families. It's been a long time, and they must be keen to see how you're getting on.'

Violet sighed. 'I've written to my dad twice already, but I might be wasting my time. I'm not sure if he's able to get letters.'

'And what about you, Tilly and Lauren?'

Suddenly I felt bad. Tilly and I knew exactly why we hadn't been in contact with our families, but Elsie couldn't possibly guess at the truth. She must have thought that we, and our families, were totally weird and heartless.

Elsie was holding a writing pad towards us. 'Do you want to write to your parents?' she asked.

I'd love to, I thought, *except I have no address, because my house isn't going to be built for another sixty years or so.*

'Thanks, Elsie,' said Tilly, 'but we're not allowed to communicate by letter. You see, both of our families are involved in war work.'

'Undercover kind of stuff,' I said, adding to her made-up story as best I could.

'Top secret,' said Tilly.

'So that's why we can't write to them, and why we haven't got any letters either,' I finished.

It sounded like a pretty pathetic explanation, but Elsie didn't seem to notice. 'Well, never you mind,' she said. 'The four of us will just be one happy family for as long as it takes.'

'Great,' said Tilly weakly. 'For as long as it takes.'

12

Another week passed, and still there was no sign of Saturn. By now, school had become unbearably boring, and I didn't think I could stand any more. 'I take back all the bad things I said about Mrs Simms,' I said one day to Tilly. 'At least she never made us spend hours putting on and taking off gas masks, and reciting what we should do in an air raid.'

'I wonder why?' said Tilly sarcastically.

'Anyway, going to school here is a total waste of our time,' I said. 'It's not like we're missing anything at home.'

'Why aren't you missing anything at home?' asked Violet, who had come over without me noticing her.

Oops! Violet was a really good friend now, and I could never get used to the fact that, basically, our whole relationship was built on a lie. (I was often tempted to tell her the truth, but Tilly and I had agreed that Violet probably wouldn't believe us and, if she did, it would totally freak her out.)

'Our school at home is very different to the one here,' I said quickly. 'And if we learn stuff here it would only confuse us when we get home.'

If we get home, came to my mind, but I pushed that awful thought away.

'I'm beginning to think that everything about your home is different to here,' said Violet. 'Sometimes it's like you two girls are from a whole different world to me.'

Tilly and I laughed big fake laughs, and I decided it was time to change the subject. 'You must be bored at school too, Violet,' I said, 'since you're so clever.'

'Yeah,' said Tilly. 'You know more than the teacher does.'

Violet went red at the compliment, but she didn't deny it.

'I'd really love to quit school,' I said.

'But would Elsie let us?' asked Tilly.

'And if she did, where would we go all day?' said Violet.

'We couldn't hang around Elsie's house,' I said. 'It wouldn't be fair on her.'

Now Tilly was smiling. 'Leave it to me, girls. I think I have a plan.'

Persuading Elsie to let us quit school was easier than any of us imagined.

'Leave school?' she said when Tilly asked her. 'Why ever not? School is greatly overrated, I think. I never went myself. I had a governess until I was fourteen.'

'But won't we get in trouble with the authorities?' I asked.

'I don't think so,' said Elsie. 'Everything is so confused, with evacuees coming and going – I don't think they'll even notice that you're missing.'

We all jumped up and hugged.

'Congratulations, girls!' said Tilly. 'Your evacuation schooldays are officially over.'

*

We had a late breakfast the next morning, and then Elsie prepared us some sandwiches and a big flask of tea. 'Where exactly are we going?' I asked as Tilly, Violet and I set off down the street. 'It's too cold for the beach, and it's not like there's a shopping centre or an omniplex nearby.'

'What's a . . .?' began Violet, but by now I was ready.

'Something we have where we come from,' I said, giving her the answer I used a hundred times a day.

'We're going to find George,' said Tilly, and then refused to say any more.

We found George digging a trench in a field near his house. 'Hey, George,' said Tilly. 'Remember what you told us about going up to The Willows every day to light fires?'

Suddenly her plan became clear, and I had to hand it to her – it was a great plan.

'Of course I remember,' said George. 'I'm going up there in a few minutes.'

Tilly smiled her sweetest smile. 'Do you think we could go with you? We've decided not to go to school any more, so we need somewhere to hang out during the daytime.'

'I'm not really sure,' said George. 'I'm not supposed to . . .'

'Pretty please?' said Violet with a shy smile.

That was all it took. Every day, George seemed more and more in love with Violet, and I had a funny feeling that if she asked him to jump into the ocean and swim to America, he'd seriously consider doing it.

'Of course you can "hang out" there,' said George. 'The Morgans wouldn't mind. I know you'll be careful, and it won't do any harm at all. Let me just finish here, and we can all go together.'

At The Willows, George opened the side door, and led us through a maze of dark corridors until we came to a huge entrance hall. It was chilly and dark and totally amazing.

'Wow,' said Tilly.

'Wow,' said Violet.

'Let's explore,' I said.

We went from room to room and, even though most of the furniture was covered with huge white sheets, it was totally cool. It was like being on the set of a movie. I was itching to see everything, but felt guilty for rushing as we waited for Violet to catch up. Much later, when we'd seen all the rooms, we went back downstairs to the library where George was lighting a fire.

Tilly took the dust sheets off the furniture and threw herself on to a couch with a big sigh. 'Pass me a book, Lauren,' she said. 'I'm not moving until it's time to go back to Elsie's house for tea.'

George finished lighting the fires, and then he checked all the doors and windows. 'I'll be back at five to lock up,' he said.

'We'll be here,' I replied and then we settled down for a lovely day of lazing and reading.

When George came back we had covered the furniture again, swept up the crumbs from our lunch, and were waiting at the front door. 'Thank you so very much,' said Violet, and George grinned like she'd given him the best present ever.

'I'll let you in again tomorrow,' he said. 'But it will have to be earlier. I'm going to school.'

I couldn't bear the thought of him sitting in that stuffy classroom, surrounded by the tiny kids and being picked on by the horrible teacher. 'Don't go to school,' I said.

'I have to,' he said. 'I need to be able to read . . . for when I join the army.'

'I'll teach you how to read,' said Violet suddenly. She must have surprised herself, as she went red and covered her mouth, almost like she regretted the words.

Too late, though. George was beaming. 'You'd do that for me?'

Violet was speechless.

'Of course she'd do that,' I said. 'After all, you helped with her swimming lessons, so she owes you.'

Violet had recovered a bit. 'I'd love to,' she

116

whispered. 'Bring your reading and writing books, and we'll start first thing in the morning.'

Early next morning we were in the library at The Willows again. 'Now that I'm not going to school, I have to do some jobs on the farm,' said George. 'But I'll be back after lunch for my reading lesson, all right?'

Violet nodded and watched dreamily as he left.

'You really like him, don't you?' I asked as soon as he had closed the door behind him.

Violet went red. 'We're just friends,' she said primly.

'For now,' said Tilly, and ducked as Violet threw a packet of sandwiches at her.

'Stop messing, you two,' I said. 'Or you'll have to go to the servants' quarters. And speaking of servants, Violet, you should have someone to carry this suitcase. It's killing me.'

'Thanks so much for carrying it all the way here,' said Violet. 'It's my maths books. I've been falling behind in my reading.'

I put the suitcase on the table and watched as Violet opened it and pulled out a stack of huge, serious-looking maths books with dusty grey covers.

'At home, my maths book has pictures of clowns on it, and is called "Maths is Fun",' I said. 'These books seem to be screaming "Maths is no fun at all".'

Violet laughed. 'Oh trust me,' she said. 'Maths is great fun – it's my favourite thing in the whole world.'

'Do you like maths more than you like George?' asked Tilly, giggling, and Violet stuck her tongue out at her.

'Anyway,' I said. 'Where did you get those books?'

'They're old university textbooks,' said Violet. 'I got them when a library near me was closing down. I know a girl like me will never go to university, but I like to read them anyway.'

'Of course a girl like you could go to university,' said Tilly.

Violet shook her head. 'I'm poor and I'm a cri–'

I glared at her and she corrected herself. 'I'm disabled.'

'You've got a weak leg,' said Tilly. 'But your amazing brain more than makes up for that. After this war, things will be different, and you'll get the opportunities you deserve. You just wait and see.'

'Do you really think so?' asked Violet with shining eyes.

'Yes,' said Tilly.

'Absolutely,' I said. 'Now start reading. You need to be ready when opportunity comes knocking on your door.'

And so the days settled into a pattern. Every morning we went to The Willows and read, played board games and chatted. Whenever George was free, he came too, and Violet spent hours teaching him to read. Every evening we went back to Elsie's place where we sat by the fire and listened to her amazing stories.

Everything would have been totally perfect except

for one small detail – Tilly and I were trapped in the wrong place, and the wrong time. As long as Saturn was lost, our real lives might as well have been a gazillion miles away.

13

'Happy Christmas, Lauren!'

I lay for a second with my eyes closed. How could it be Christmas? How could it possibly be Christmas when I was so far away from Mum and Dad and Amy and Stephen? I could feel tears beginning, but held them back. I'd been crying far too much lately.

Now Tilly was shaking my arm. 'Wake up, Lauren,' she said. 'I've got you a present.'

I sat up and shivered. Once again, ice had made swirly white patterns on the inside of our bedroom window. They were pretty, but I'd have happily exchanged them for a big warm radiator.

Tilly was sitting up in bed too, holding a package

out to me. 'I know you need a phone but the village shop was all out of them so I got you this instead.'

I unwrapped a small packet of toffees and smiled as I handed her an identical packet, wrapped up in second-hand tissue paper.

'Elsie lent me the money,' I said. 'Otherwise I wouldn't have been able to get you anything at all.'

'Same here,' said Tilly. 'Good old Elsie.'

Tilly unwrapped her present and laughed when she saw the toffees. 'Great minds think alike,' she said. 'And, besides, that was all the shop had when I went there.'

'Me too,' I said sadly.

Lately, the local shop had mostly empty shelves, and even though we never went hungry, the food we ate was becoming really boring and repetitive. Elsie said we shouldn't complain as things were much worse in the cities. I knew she was right, but still I couldn't help thinking of the loaded supermarket shelves I was used to at home.

Now Tilly hugged me. 'Don't be sad, Lauren,' she said.

I hugged her back. 'I can't help being sad. We've been stuck here for nearly four months now, and even I have to accept that Saturn probably isn't going to come back.'

'Saturn isn't just any old cat,' said Tilly. 'He's special. He's magical. I know he'd never abandon us. I bet he's got a plan – he just didn't share it with us, that's all.'

As always, Tilly's pep-talk made me feel a bit better, and then I thought of something else.

'Everyone only gets a certain amount of Christmases in their lives, so this is like a bonus. Who ever knew that we'd get to celebrate Christmas 1939?'

'That's the spirit,' said Tilly. 'Now hurry and get dressed. I've got some packets of toffees to give to Violet and Elsie!'

When we went downstairs we huddled round the living-room fire, trying to get warm. Elsie gave us each a tiny book she had made, containing one of her stories, illustrated with watercolour pictures. Then we all laughed as Violet gave everyone a small packet of toffees.

'Don't laugh too much,' said Elsie. 'There's a war on, and we have to be grateful for every little thing we get. I fear that things are going to get worse before they get better.'

'I refuse to think bad thoughts on Christmas Day,' said Violet. 'Now excuse me while I go to read my father's letter. I'm dying to see what he's got to say.'

'But that letter came two days ago,' said Elsie.

'I know,' said Violet. 'I've been saving it.'

She went back into her bedroom, and Elsie gazed at us sadly. 'You two poor girls,' she said. 'All this time and your parents haven't been able to write to you.'

'Oh, don't worry about it,' Tilly said. 'It's always like that when we're away from home. We're used to it by now.'

'And what about Arthur?' I asked.

Elsie shook her head sadly. 'Twenty-five years, and he's never had a Christmas without me – until now.'

'That's so sad,' said Tilly.

Elsie smiled a brave smile. 'Yes, it is sad, but he's

doing very important work, so I shouldn't complain. And hopefully he'll be home on leave before too long, and you can all get to know him.'

We had a really nice Christmas Day, but I had to keep reminding myself that I wasn't missing Christmas at home. As far as I knew (and hoped), it was still an ordinary Friday afternoon there, and there weren't search parties out for Tilly and me – even though we'd just spent months and months in England in 1939.

Later on, Elsie cooked a special Christmas dinner, with a chicken from George's farm, and potatoes and vegetables she had got from another local farmer.

'I couldn't get Christmas crackers,' said Elsie, 'so I had to improvise.' We giggled as she produced twists of newspaper, painted bright red. She hadn't been able to improvise bangers, so we had great fun trying to shout 'bang' at the correct moment, just before the cracker split and a toffee and a poem by Elsie fell out.

We all did our best to be happy, even though Elsie

was missing her son, and Violet was missing her dad, and Tilly and I were very, very much missing our families.

After lunch, George called over with a cake his mother had made and a card. He smiled shyly as Violet opened the card and read the message aloud.

To my dear friends, Violet, Tilly and Lauren.
Happy Christmas and may all good things come to you in 1940.

'I wrote it myself,' he said proudly.

Violet shook his hand formally, but I couldn't even force a smile. Were Tilly and I going to have to live through 1940? And 1941? And all the years after that?

Were our real lives lost forever?

 **14**

'Come along, girls. We all have to do our bit.
And it can't be that hard – people have been
growing vegetables for centuries.'

'Don't worry, Elsie,' said Tilly. 'Lauren has
gardening experience.'

'Tell us more, Lauren,' said Elsie.

'Er . . . I've forgotten most of it,' I said. 'It was
kind of a long time ago.'

I glared at Tilly. How could I possibly explain
that my experience of growing vegetables was when
I was a slave in Pompeii in the year 79?

Recently posters had appeared all over the village,
showing a man carrying a big basket of vegetables
and the words – DIG FOR VICTORY. 'It's our

small part in the war effort,' explained Elsie as she handed us each a gardening tool. 'We can't fight for our country, but if we provide some of our own food, we will at least be doing something to help.'

'And I read up on gardening in the library in The Willows,' said Violet. 'March is the perfect time for sowing seeds.'

I already knew what month it was, of course, but hearing Violet saying it, made my stomach lurch. Tilly and I had now been trapped in the past for over six months, and the scariness of that was never far away.

I often cried myself to sleep thinking of Mum and Dad and Amy and Stephen. Time wasn't passing for them, but, for me, being away from them was getting harder and harder each day. Sometimes, when I woke up in the morning, my eyes were red and swollen, and even Tilly's consoling hugs couldn't make me feel better.

It took the whole morning to clear a small patch of ground. Once that was done, we followed Violet's instructions and sowed some carrots, turnips and cabbages. When we were finished, Tilly and I went to buy sugar and butter for Violet's birthday cake.

'Are you sorry about keeping your birthday a secret last week?' I asked as we walked.

She shook her head. 'No, I'm not sorry. It was weird but I'm glad we did it that way.'

'It must have been hard though. I know how your dad always tries to make your birthday special.'

She gave a small, sad smile. 'I did miss Dad a lot that day. But you were nice. It was really generous of you to give me your last few toffees. And I know I was doing the right thing by not telling Elsie and Violet. How could I celebrate my thirteenth birthday here, and yet still be twelve when I get home?'

'What if –' I began, but she interrupted me.

'We're going home, Lauren,' she said firmly. 'I don't know when, but I know it's going to happen.'

I didn't argue. It's nice having a friend when you're in trouble. When one of us was down and upset it was the other person's job to be upbeat and hopeful – it was our best way of surviving.

At the shop we watched the shopkeeper as he carefully weighed out the sugar and butter, and marked the amounts in our ration books.

'I'll never get used to this,' I said as we took the two small bags and walked out of the shop. 'How is this meant to last four of us for a whole week?'

Tilly sighed. 'And most of it will be used for Violet's cake.'

'Lucky Elsie's good at making cakes then,' I said. 'If she made a mess and wasted all this precious food, I don't think I could ever forgive her.'

I thought longingly of Mum's baking cupboard at home. She has jars and jars of sugar – brown, white, icing, caster – and other weird ones I didn't know the name of.

Why hadn't I ever appreciated how lucky we were?

The next day we all sat round the table, singing 'Happy Birthday' to Violet. We didn't have any candles, so Elsie used some of our precious oil supply to light the oil lamp and let Violet blow that out instead.

Elsie went to get a knife, and my mouth was watering at the thought of biting into the cake, when the front door was suddenly flung open and I heard a loud happy voice. 'I'm home! What's for tea?'

Elsie gave a little squeal and raced into the tiny hall. We followed to find her tightly wrapped in the arms of a huge, tall, uniformed man.

'You naughty boy,' Elsie was saying to this man who was about three times her size. 'Why didn't you tell me you were coming home?'

The man winked at us over the top of Elsie's head. 'Well, Mother, if you'd told me the house was full of such lovely ladies, I'd have been home months ago.'

He'd only been in the house for a few minutes, but already I liked this tall man with the twinkly eyes and smiling face, who was very obviously Elsie's only son, and her pride and joy.

He finally released his mother and she turned round to do the formal introductions. She was breathless and tearful, and it looked like she was going to burst from happiness.

131

Tilly made tea and we all sat down to tea and cake.

'This cake is totally delicious,' I said. 'Thanks, Elsie.'

She smiled. 'You are very welcome, dear. But make the most of it, because that's our sugar ration used up, and there won't be anything else sweet until next week.'

'That's what you think, Mother,' said Arthur. He reached into his bag and pulled out a big bar of chocolate. He put it on the table, and we all stared at it like it was the most precious thing we'd ever seen. I reached out and touched it, half afraid that it was an illusion.

'Omigod,' said Tilly. 'Chocolate.'

'I thought I was never going to see chocolate again,' sighed Violet.

Elsie stood and picked up the chocolate. She cleared a space between the photos of Arthur and her husband on the mantelpiece, and carefully laid the chocolate down.

'We're keeping this until Sunday,' she said. 'For a special treat.'

Arthur smiled, looking a bit embarrassed at the fuss he had caused.

Elsie came back to the table and stood by him. 'I worry so much about you when you are away,' she said.

'But I write every week.' He sounded like a little boy, trying not to be in trouble with his mum.

She patted his hand. 'I know you do, but by the time the army censor is finished cutting pieces out of your letters, there's not much left. It looks like you're writing on lace.'

Arthur smiled. 'You know how important secrecy is, Mother. Anyway, I have some good news. I'm not going back to France. I've got a new posting – in England.'

Elsie hugged him. 'Oh, my dear boy,' she said. 'That *is* good news. What will you be doing, and where will you be based?'

'Mother!' he said, shocked. 'You know I can't tell you the details. It's undercover work and top secret. All I can tell you is that I won't be too far away. I'll be in Bletchley Park, in Buckinghamshire.'

'Oh,' said Tilly. 'I know about that place. You're going to be a code-breaker then? That's so cool.'

'What's a code-breaker?' I asked.

'The code-breakers crack the enemy's top-secret codes so they know in advance what they're going to do,' said Tilly, showing off a bit. 'Some people think code-breakers were the ones who really won the war.'

I looked at her in amazement. 'How do you know all that?' I asked.

She leaned over and whispered in my ear. 'I saw a film about it on TV once.'

I was starting to laugh, when I turned to look at Arthur. All the colour had drained from his face and he was looking over his shoulder like a team of sergeant-majors was going to appear and lock him up forever.

'Highest secrecy level,' he muttered. 'Need-to-know basis. The safety of our entire nation is at stake.' Then he turned and stared at Tilly. All traces of the smiling, twinkly man were gone. 'Who told you about our work in Bletchley Park?' he asked in a stern, scary voice.

Now Tilly's face had gone equally pale. 'It was just a lucky guess,' she squeaked. 'And I won't tell anyone, I promise.'

Arthur gave us all a serious lecture on how important it was not to say stuff that could help the enemy. I didn't figure it likely that there was an enemy hiding under the table in Elsie's living room, but decided not to point that out.

'I am really, really sorry, Arthur,' said Tilly, who looked a bit shaken. 'I should have known better. *Tittle tattle lost the battle*, and *loose lips sink ships*, all that stuff.'

Elsie looked embarrassed by what had just happened. 'Those would be good slogans,' she said. 'They should put them on posters.'

The look on Tilly's face made me sure that they probably *were* going to do exactly that.

After a while, Arthur relaxed again, and we enjoyed the rest of the party.

Arthur needed somewhere to sleep, so that night Violet moved up to share the room that Tilly and I were using. It was a bit uncomfortable with three of

135

us squashed into the small bed, but Violet didn't seem to mind. 'It's like having sisters,' she said. 'I've always wanted a sister.'

'Me too,' said Tilly.

'Trust me, sisters aren't all they're cracked up to be,' I said quickly, but then I felt bad as I realized how much I'd like to be at home with Amy and the rest of my family.

Violet snuggled between Tilly and me with a big contented sigh. I had the horrible feeling that, even though we were in the middle of a war, Violet was experiencing the happiest days she'd known for a very long time.

 **15**

Arthur's visit livened us all up for a while, but when he left a few days later everything seemed dull and boring. Time passed slowly and I felt like a prisoner, ticking off days on a mental chart – except that, unlike a prisoner, I had no idea when, if ever, I was going to be free to go back to my old life. Saturn was my jailer, and it looked like he had vanished with the key of my cell.

We still went to The Willows every day – mostly because there was nowhere else to go. Violet was an amazing teacher and, now that no one was calling him stupid, George was turning out to be really clever. He had graduated from ABC books, and was now making his way through the complete works of Charles Dickens.

The novelty of rationing had worn off months ago, and I thought that if I saw an orange or a banana I might faint away from excitement. The vegetables we had sown were growing well, which was kind of cool, but they weren't ready to eat yet. I couldn't help thinking that if only Tilly and I could have popped home and whizzed a trolley around our local supermarket, we could have saved ourselves a whole lot of trouble.

Then one day near the end of May, George called over. 'Have you heard the radio reports?' he said. 'It looks like our army is in a lot of trouble in France. They're retreating.'

We had heard the stories and, since Violet's father was somewhere in France, we were all very worried. Also, I had a horrible feeling that the radio was making things sound better than they were, and that the reality was far worse than Violet or George could ever have guessed.

'It's so frustrating,' said George. 'I'm tall and

strong, and I should be out there with the other men.'

'You've tried your hardest,' said Violet.

She was right there. Once every few weeks, George packed up and tried to enlist, but every time, he was turned away for being too young.

'I have to do something to help. I just have to,' said George.

I knew that talk of growing vegetables and milking cows wasn't going to console him, so I just patted his arm and tried to understand how he felt.

A few days later, Tilly, Violet and I were at The Willows as usual, when George appeared. Violet picked up the book he had been reading, and held it out to him. 'Here, George,' she said. 'I've marked your page for you.'

He pushed the book away. 'Thanks, Violet, but this isn't the time for reading. This is the time for action.'

'I know, but –' began Violet.

George put up his hand to stop her. 'Our troops have been pushed right back to the coast in France,' he said. 'They're trapped on the beaches in a place called Dunkirk. They are all lined up, waiting to be rescued, but there are thousands and thousands of them, and not enough boats.'

'That's very scary,' said Tilly. 'But what's it got to do with us?'

Now George looked even more determined. 'I know someone who has been to the big port a few miles from here. He said that civilians have been called on to help. People with boats have been asked to sail across the Channel to rescue our men.'

'I still don't get it,' said Tilly.

'It's not like we have a boat or anything,' I said.

George's face was pale and grim. 'Just follow me,' he said.

The three of us followed him out of the house and down a narrow path to a wooden building on the edge of the water. We passed close to the building almost every day, but I'd never paid it a whole lot of attention before.

'What's this old shed got to do with anything?' asked Tilly.

'It's not a shed,' said George, smiling for the first time. 'It's a boathouse. And I've got the key.'

George opened the creaky door and led us into a gloomy, cobwebby space. There, up on a wooden stand, was a large boat with a bright red stripe painted all round it.

'Who owns this?' I asked weakly.

'It belongs to the Morgans. I know they won't mind me using it – since it's for such a good cause.'

'And do you know *how* to drive it . . . or sail it . . . or you know . . . make it go places?' I asked.

George nodded. 'I often go out with the Morgan family when they're going fishing. I know exactly what to do.'

'But fuel is rationed,' said Tilly. 'And we haven't got any.'

George pointed to a storage tank in the corner of the boathouse. 'The Morgans always keep some here. There'll be plenty – there always is.'

There was a long silence.

Sitting out the war in the countryside wasn't scary at all. Boring yes, but scary no. But now, George, our friend, was planning to sail right into the middle of a battle. There would be guns and bombs and tanks. Where George wanted to go, the soldiers wouldn't be clean and smiley like Arthur – they'd be dirty and wet and cold and wounded. There was a very real danger that if George went off in that boat, we might never see him again.

'That's a very big boat,' I said in the end. 'Surely you can't manage it on your own.'

'That's why I've asked my cousin Harry to come along with me,' said George. 'He should be here any minute.'

Violet stepped forward. 'My father could be one of those men waiting to be rescued,' she said. 'I know I'm disabled, but I'm not a coward. I want to go with you too.'

George looked embarrassed. 'I'm sorry, Violet,' he said gently, 'but you wouldn't be strong enough to pull soldiers on board.'

Violet put her head down. 'I should have known I'd be useless,' she said.

I didn't know what to say to this, so I just hugged her, wondering if that made any difference at all.

George was already opening the huge door that led from the boathouse to the water. 'Come and help,' he said. 'We need to have the boat ready for when Harry gets here. A few lost seconds will cost us hours in the end.'

'How come?' asked Tilly.

George pointed across the water. 'There's a sandbar out there, and this boat won't make it past at low tide. If we don't go soon, the water will be too low, and we'll have to wait hours and hours before it's high enough again.'

It took the four of us a long time to manoeuvre the boat down the wooden ramps and into the water. George tied it firmly to a large metal ring set into the slipway. He spent ages checking the fuel tanks and then Tilly helped him to load up large drums of spare fuel. Violet searched the boathouse for life jackets and waterproof gear, and I raced back to The

Willows to get the big packet of sandwiches and flask of tea that Elsie had given us that morning.

George took the food and the flask and climbed aboard. And then we waited.

And waited.

16

Twenty minutes later, we were still waiting.

Tilly, Violet and I were sitting on the slipway and George was standing on the boat, anxiously watching for his cousin.

I tried to make small talk – not easy in the circumstances. 'Do you actually know the way to France, George?' I asked.

'I'll be able to work it out. Mr Morgan doesn't cut corners. This boat was fully refitted in 1937 – so it's completely modern. I've got the best equipment money can buy and a cupboard full of charts.'

'And how long will you be gone?' I asked.

George looked grim. 'Hard to say,' he said. 'We'll be home when the job is done.'

'You're so brave,' sighed Violet. She'd never seen a war movie, and I suspected she had no idea what kind of situation George was headed for.

Five more minutes passed, and the water was slipping lower and lower on the shingly beach. Still there was no sign of Harry.

'Something must have happened to him,' said George. 'If he's not here in the next ten minutes, I'm going to have to go without him.'

'But you can't go on your own!' I said.

He shrugged. 'Has either of you two got any experience of boats?'

'I went on a pedal-boat in Majorca once,' I said with a nervous giggle. 'I crashed it.'

George and Violet stared at me, and I guessed that they'd never heard of Majorca, and hadn't the faintest idea what a pedal-boat was.

'Totally pathetic, Lauren,' said Tilly. 'My cousin in Galway has a boat, and I've been out on it with her heaps of times. And, besides, I'm a stronger swimmer than you. It's decided. I'll go with George.'

This sooo didn't seem right. Tilly was my best friend. We were supposed to do stuff like going to the cinema and hanging around shopping malls. How could I just watch her sail into the middle of a war?

'Hang on a sec, George,' I said. 'You can't just leave like this. Shouldn't you go to the port and register? Shouldn't lots of boats travel together? You know, safety in numbers and all that stuff.'

For the first time, George looked uncertain. 'Yes, you're right, Lauren. We should register with the navy, but how can we do that? Technically, this boat is stolen, and it's being sailed by a child. If we try to register, they won't let us go. Don't worry, the call for help went out last Friday, so boats have been doing this for days and days. They've found a safe way through the mines.'

I gulped. 'There are mines?' I squeaked.

George didn't answer my question. 'Once we get into the open water,' he said, 'we'll see the other boats. We can join up with them then – when it's too late for anyone to do anything about it.'

For a single second, I let myself be carried away by the excitement and drama of it all, and then the reality hit me. 'No!' I said. 'I'm not letting you go, Tilly. It's crazy and it's dangerous.'

Tilly didn't answer.

George started the boat's engine, and looked at Tilly. 'Well?' he said.

'She's not going,' I said.

Still Tilly didn't move.

I caught her shoulders and stared into her face. 'I know you want to help, Tilly, but you can't. This isn't some romantic movie. This is real life, and a real war. It's too dangerous, and I can't let you do it.'

Tilly didn't reply, so I released her and turned to Violet for help. 'This is too mad and scary,' I said. 'Tell her, Violet.'

But Violet didn't speak either. She looked at me, then Tilly, before she gazed out to sea. At last I understood. How would I feel if it was *my* father trapped at the edge of the war?

But Tilly was my friend, and my responsibility. I

grabbed her arm. 'You're not going,' I said. 'Sorry.'

'I'm sorry too,' she whispered, and I relaxed my grip, glad that she was seeing sense. But in one movement she was free. She untied the rope and leapt into the boat, pushing off against the slipway with her feet.

'Go, George,' she said, and he obediently revved the engines. I dived for the trailing rope, but it slithered out of my hands, spraying my face with cold seaweedy water. As the boat slipped away, I scrambled to my feet and raced uselessly after it, stumbling on the rocky shore.

George and Tilly stared back at us. Tilly was pale, but determined-looking. 'Bye, Lauren! Bye, Violet!' she called. 'Don't worry about us. We'll be home before you know it.'

'Come back, Tilly!' I shouted. 'Please come back.'

Her only reply was a slight shake of her head.

This was the worst thing that had ever happened to me.

I thought of all the scary war movies I'd ever watched.

I thought of the terrible things that lay ahead of Tilly.

How could I survive in 1940 without my best friend there to make it sort of all right?

How could Tilly do this to herself?

How could she do this to me?

'I hate you, Tilly!' I screamed across the water. 'I really, really hate you!' The wind whipped the words from my mouth, but even so, I knew that Tilly had heard me.

I turned and ran back to where Violet was still standing at the edge of the slipway. I threw myself into her arms and she hugged me tight. Then she patted my back as I sobbed desperately, while our two dear friends vanished into the distance.

17

Violet and I stood on the shore for a long time, looking out across the empty water. 'Do you have any idea how long it takes to get to France?' asked Violet after a while.

I knew that in a plane you could probably do it in an hour or two, but since Tilly and George were in a boat that wasn't a whole lot of help. 'I have no idea.'

'Anyway, we shouldn't expect them back before tomorrow – or maybe even the day after.'

I gasped at the thought of all that time without Tilly, and then I thought of something else. 'We've got to go home later on,' I said, 'and Tilly's not going to be with us. How are we going to explain that to Elsie?'

'We could tell her the truth?'

I shook my head. 'No, that wouldn't be fair. It's too late to stop Tilly, so there's no point in making Elsie worry when there's not a single thing she can do about it.'

'So what *will* we tell her?'

I thought for a minute. 'I know,' I said in the end. 'Remember what happened to Gerald, the boy in our class, a few weeks ago?'

'Is he the one who left suddenly?'

'Yes,' I said. 'And all we have to do is steal his story. We'll tell Elsie that Tilly's granny is really sick, and that her aunt came to pick her up and take her to London to visit her.'

'And, just like Gerald, Tilly will be back in a few days, and everything will be fine.' Did she really believe this, or was she just trying to make me feel better?

I sighed. 'I really, really hope you're right.'

We stood and watched the empty sea for another while, and then, because I could see that Violet was shivering in the breeze, I insisted that we go back to The Willows.

Violet seemed to walk even slower and more awkwardly than usual. 'I'm useless,' she said. 'Completely useless. Tilly and George are doing such a great thing, and here I am, doing nothing.'

'I'm not doing a whole lot either,' I pointed out.

'But you could,' said Violet. 'And that's the difference. If George had a bigger boat, you could have gone too. But even if he had an ocean liner, there's nothing I could do. I'm no good to anyone – and I never will be.'

She put her head down, and I slipped an arm round her shoulders, hating myself because I couldn't think of a single thing to say to make her feel better.

When we got to The Willows I used the key George had given us and we went to our usual spot in the library. Without Tilly and George, though, everything felt strange and lonely. How could we relax and read while Tilly and George were far away, risking their lives?

In the end the silence got to me. 'This is just too creepy,' I said. 'Will I get one of your maths books for you?'

Violet shook her head. 'I've finished them all. I think I know every single word of them. And I've checked all the shelves here. Whoever set up this library wasn't a big maths enthusiast.'

Then I thought of something. I went into the small storeroom off the kitchen, and picked up a bundle of old newspapers that I'd seen there.

'What are those for?' asked Violet as I dropped them at her feet. 'They are all months out of date.'

'Cryptic crosswords,' I said. 'My mum is great at maths and she loves cryptic crosswords, so I bet you would too.'

I found two consecutive newspapers, and tore out the crosswords and solutions. 'Here,' I said as I handed them to her, 'you can read the clues, and then the answers from the next day's paper – just so you can see how they work.'

Violet studied a crossword and the answers for a long time. A few times she sighed and scratched her head. Twice she said 'Oh fiddlesticks!' so crossly that I was tempted to laugh. After a while, I was beginning to think that maybe she wasn't as clever as I had imagined, when she suddenly sat up straight and smiled.

'I've got the hang of it now. Would you mind passing me a pencil, please, Lauren? I want to test myself.'

I got her a pencil and a new crossword from the pile. Then I went and selected a book for myself from the shelves. I had only read a few pages when Violet passed the crossword to me. 'Done,' she said triumphantly. 'Do you want to check it?'

I gasped. 'That can't have taken you more than ten minutes. My mum has been doing this for years, and even on a good day, it takes her most of an hour.'

'Probably beginner's luck,' said Violet.

'One way of finding out,' I said, as I found another crossword and handed it to her.

This time Violet finished even quicker than before.

'That is totally amazing,' I said when I'd checked the answers. 'Do you have any idea how hard most people find those crosswords? You're like a genius or something.'

Violet smiled, but it quickly faded. 'Crosswords are fun,' she said. 'But they'll never save lives. I'd prefer to be able to do something useful.'

I was too worried about Tilly and George to argue properly, so I gave up and read my book while Violet flicked through the papers, and we both waited for time to pass.

I was glad when it was six o'clock and we could go back to Elsie's house for tea.

Tiddles rubbed up against my leg as we walked into the front garden but I pushed him away. Maybe all this was his fault. If he hadn't scared Saturn away, then Tilly and I wouldn't have got trapped in 1940. And if we weren't trapped in 1940, then Tilly wouldn't be off risking her life in a tiny boat on a huge sea. Tiddles gave a hurt miaow and went to sit on the garden wall.

'Where's Tilly?' asked Elsie when we walked in.

I gave the answer Violet and I had prepared, and Elsie was immediately sympathetic.

'Oh poor Tilly,' she said. 'Why didn't she come

back and tell me? She and her aunt could have had a nice cup of tea, and I could have given them sandwiches for the journey.'

Now I felt really bad. If only Tilly really was on a nice train journey with her aunt, instead of off on a mad, dangerous adventure.

'Oh, they'd have loved that,' I said quickly, 'but they were rushing to catch the train.'

I wondered if Elsie was going to believe my made-up story, but then she smiled and I knew she had something else on her mind.

'I got a letter,' she said. 'From Arthur. He's coming home on leave. He'll be here in a few days. He'll be so pleased to see you three lovely girls again.'

I tried to look happy. Meeting Arthur would be nice, but I very much hoped that when he arrived, there *would* be three lovely girls here for him to see.

 18

The next day was the slowest and most horrible of my whole life. Violet and I spent hours standing on the shore near the boathouse, watching the sea. Sometimes I looked for so long that I felt dizzy and sick. No matter how long I looked, though, it didn't make any difference – there was no sign of my friends.

'You know what the worst thing is?' I said, sometime in the afternoon.

'What?' asked Violet.

'I told Tilly that I hate her,' I said. 'And what if she doesn't come back? What if those are the last words I'll ever get to say to her?' The very thought of it brought tears to my eyes for the hundredth time that day.

Violet hugged me. 'You were angry and scared,' she said. 'You didn't mean it. And, anyway, Tilly's coming back and, when she does, you can say hundreds and thousands of nice things to her.'

Then I thought of something else. 'If . . . if Tilly and George . . . if . . . if something terrible happens to them, we'll never even know. There's a war on, and no one will have time to find out what happened to one small boat. You and I could just stand here waiting forever – or until we finally give up hope and accept the awful truth.'

Violet tried to be positive. 'George will bring Tilly back,' she said. 'He's big and strong and brave. Remember how he rescued us from all those bullies?'

That didn't make me feel any better. Saving us from little boys with sticks was one thing, but not quite the same as battling mines and guns and bombs and bullets.

We stayed by the shore until it was dark. I wanted to stay even longer, but Violet pulled me away. 'We should go home,' she said. 'Wherever George and Tilly are, they'll probably stay till morning. And we'll be at the boathouse first thing to welcome them. You'll see. Everything is better after a night's sleep.'

But Violet was wrong. After hours of broken, nightmare-filled sleep, I felt even worse than before. I woke early and looked across the bed to where Tilly usually lay, and I gave a hoarse sob. Soon tears were rolling down my cheeks and on to the lace bedspread. Was my best friend gone forever?

Suddenly I didn't care about Saturn any more. I'd happily live forever in the past, if only my friend would come back, safe and well.

When I went downstairs, Elsie dabbed at my red eyes with a lace hanky. 'You poor little dear,' she whispered. 'I know how close you and Tilly are, but try not to be sad. I'm sure her Granny will be better soon. You mark my words, Tilly will be back with us before you know it.'

That made me cry even more. Elsie hugged me, then she sat me at the table and made me tea and fussed over me. She probably thought I was a complete loser, being so upset about my friend going to London for a few days.

I couldn't touch the breakfast Elsie had prepared, and as soon as Violet was ready, we walked to the boathouse. I know it was mean of me, but I couldn't help being irritated that Violet was so slow. I didn't say anything, but she saw how impatient I was.

'You run on ahead,' she said. 'I don't mind.'

But when it came to it, I didn't move any faster. Since George and Tilly were unlikely to be there, what was all the rush in aid of?

So I walked at Violet's slow pace and when we got to the boathouse, things were exactly as I had expected. The calm grey water stretched out to the horizon, and no boat appeared to brighten the view.

161

I sat on the edge of the slipway and waited.

Violet sat beside me, but we didn't talk. Yesterday we had said all we needed to say, and I had no words left.

I picked up a few pebbles and tossed them into the water, one by one. I watched as the rings they made radiated outwards – would those ripples keep going until they got to France?

And what would they find when they got there?

Hours passed. Violet unwrapped the sandwiches that Elsie had made and held one out to me. I shook my head and Violet rewrapped the food. I felt sure I would choke if I tried to eat, and, besides, eating seemed wrong at a time like this.

And then, as I picked up yet another pebble, Violet grabbed my arm.

'Look,' she said, pointing.

I followed her finger, but couldn't see anything at first. Then, ever so slowly, my eyes began to focus on a distant dark object.

Could that be a boat?

Could it be George and Tilly's boat?

I stood up and screamed and threw my arms in the air like a mad person. Violet waved her crutch so violently I thought she was going to tumble into the water.

Gradually, like it was going in the slowest of slow motion, the object came closer, and I could see that it was a boat.

Then I could see a distinctive red stripe.

Then, what felt like hours later, I could see two figures – two figures that looked alive and well and were waving madly back at us.

'They're safe,' breathed Violet.

And then she said sadly, 'But there's no one else in the boat. They didn't save anyone.'

I had a horrible feeling that she had somehow expected George and Tilly to find her dad among all the thousands of soldiers and bring him safely home to her.

Then she smiled. 'I know they did their very best. And somewhere out there, someone else did their very best too, and managed to rescue my dad.'

Minutes later, the boat was drawing up, and George was throwing the rope so I could tie it to the slipway again.

Tilly looked pale and tired, but she was beaming. 'Are you OK?' I asked.

She nodded. 'I'm fine – but that has to be the scariest thing I have ever done in my whole entire life.'

I did my best to hold the boat steady while George and Tilly climbed out. Tilly and I hugged for a long time.

'I'm so sorry for saying I hate you,' I said. 'You're mad, and what you did was totally, totally stupid, but I don't hate you.'

She grinned. 'Good,' she said. 'And I don't hate you either.' Then she turned and hugged Violet. George watched shyly until the hug-fest was over.

'So what happened?' I asked. 'Tell us everything.'

'It was terrifying but brilliant,' said Tilly. 'We saved so many men.'

I wondered if shock and exhaustion had made her hallucinate. If they'd saved so many men, then where on earth were they? 'Er, Tilly . . .?' I began.

'Now that we're on dry land, my legs feel terribly wobbly,' said Tilly. 'So let's sit down, and I'll explain from the beginning.'

We all sat on the grass at the side of the boathouse and she started to talk. It was like she was filled with nervous energy, and, once she started, she couldn't stop. 'After we left you, it didn't take long until we were out in the open water, and, like George predicted, there were loads and loads of boats. It was like some kind of weird regatta, except no one seemed to be having a whole lot of fun. And then we saw this huge tanker, and it threw us a line, so we turned off our engine and let it tow us.'

'That was to save fuel,' said George.

'And the tanker was pulling loads and loads of boats, a bit like an old lady with heaps of dogs on leads,' continued Tilly. 'I was afraid we'd all get tangled up, which so wouldn't have been funny.'

'But that didn't happen,' added George.

'No,' said Tilly. 'Anyway, the tanker pulled us for ages and ages, and George and I were just kind of sitting there like a prince and princess or something, and then when we got close to France, even though it should have been getting dark, there was all this bright light.'

'Fires,' explained George.

'And it looked like there was a huge army of ants on the beach, but as we got closer we could see that it was soldiers: thousands and thousands of them. And there were some huge ships there, but they couldn't get close to the shore, so that's why we were needed.'

'Because small boats like this can go almost right on to the beach,' said George.

It was like George and Tilly were some kind of double act, which would have been funny, except that the story they were telling us was so serious.

'So we started our engine, and left the tanker, and went right up to the beach,' said Tilly. 'And it was really scary, because there were explosions all around us, but the soldiers were so polite they kind of calmed us down. They were queuing up in the water, like they were just waiting for a bus to take them shopping or something. And when we got close, I took charge of the engine and George helped six men to climb on to our boat, and we turned round and brought them out to one of the big ships, and then we went back for more. And that's what we did, for hours and hours, and day and night. And I have *no* idea how long it went on for. What time is it anyway? What day is it anyway?'

'It's Tuesday,' I said.

'And it's around four o'clock,' said Violet.

'Omigod,' said Tilly. 'We were gone for two days.'

'Lucky you brought food with you,' I said.

Tilly grinned. 'We didn't eat it. Some of the soldiers hadn't had anything proper to eat for days, and they were totally glad when they saw our sandwiches. And when I handed one of them the flask of tea, he started to cry.'

'The poor man kept apologizing,' said George,

'He kept on saying that he'd never shed a tear before, even though he'd seen such terrible things in France, and he couldn't understand why a simple cup of tea was making him cry.'

We were all quiet for a minute. I tried to picture the scenes that Tilly and George had witnessed but it was too hard, too incredible.

'Some sailors on one of the big ships gave us food after that, though,' said George. 'They said that if we didn't eat, we'd be no good to anyone.'

'I have no idea how many men we saved,' said Tilly. 'But it was heaps and heaps.'

'My father?' breathed Violet.

Tilly leaned over and hugged her. 'He could have been in our boat, for all I know. There was no time for introductions or anything. But I bet he was rescued, Violet. There were hundreds of boats, and everyone did all they could.'

'And, finally, we were told that all the British soldiers were safe, so the order was given to come back home,' said George.

'So that's what we did,' said Tilly. 'And here we

are, and I'm starving. Have you got any food?'

'Of course,' said Violet, handing her a packet of sandwiches.

'Good old Elsie,' said Tilly.

I gave a happy sigh, hardly able to believe that my friend was safe again, sitting right in front of me, stuffing her face with cheese sandwiches. George and Violet were whispering together, so I took the opportunity to have a quiet word with Tilly. 'I'm glad you saved so many people,' I said, 'but it doesn't change the fact that going off with George was a totally crazy thing to do.'

She nodded. 'I know. It was just a sudden decision. George said he had to go, and I jumped into the boat without really thinking about what I was doing. I've read the history books, and if I'd had time to think about it properly I don't think I'd have gone at all. Anyway, it all worked out OK in the end, so who's complaining? Now, is there anything to drink around here?'

I walked down to the slipway to get the flask, but by the time I came back Tilly was stretched out on the grass, sound asleep, with a half-eaten sandwich still in her hand.

'It was a long few days,' said George, before he slid downwards too and fell into a sound sleep.

Violet and I sat and watched them with huge happy smiles on our faces.

19

Later, George stayed in the boathouse to repair a few small holes in the boat, and the rest of us made our way back to Elsie's house. When we got there, Arthur had just arrived, and he was sitting at the table being fussed over by his mother.

Elsie jumped up and hugged Tilly. 'You're back!' she said. 'And how is your poor dear grandmother?'

'I told Elsie how sick she was,' I said quickly. 'And that's why you had to go to London for a few days.'

Tilly copped on really fast. 'Oh, she's much better now,' she said. 'She's like a young girl again.'

I grinned. At that moment, Tilly's grandmother probably *was* a young girl.

'I am very glad to hear it,' said Elsie. Then she

went into the kitchen and returned with a small cake. 'Sorry, girls,' she said. 'That's another week's rations gone – so make sure you all get a slice.'

Arthur reached into his bag, and we all held our breath. Was there any chance that he had brought more chocolate?

'Sorry,' he said, as if he could read four minds at once. 'I tried everywhere but I couldn't find any chocolate, so I brought something else instead.'

As he said this, he pulled out a brown paper bag. We passed it around, and each of us peeped inside reverently, like this was the most precious thing we had ever seen.

'Sugar,' sighed Tilly. 'Who knew I'd ever be so excited by a bag of sugar?'

When we'd all spent enough time gazing at the sugar, Elsie took it and put it safely in a tin on the mantelpiece, and we all settled down for tea and cake.

After dinner and another cosy evening of Elsie's stories, everyone went to bed. Once again, Violet was sharing a room with Tilly and me, and the three of us made ourselves as comfortable as possible in the small bed. Tilly fell asleep at once and Violet followed soon afterwards. I lay awake for a long time. The moon was shining through the attic window, casting its light on the sleeping faces of my friends. It was all kind of peaceful and nice but I couldn't help thinking – is this it? – for the rest of my life?

Next morning, for a big treat, Elsie made pancakes with eggs she'd got from a neighbour. She took out the precious bag of sugar, and carefully sprinkled a few grains on to each plate. I'd have given anything for a slice of lemon to squeeze over my pancake too, but I knew that was impossible. As far as I knew, I hadn't been within a hundred miles of a lemon or an orange in months.

Afterwards, we spread rugs on the grass in the front garden, and lay outside in the pleasant sunshine. Arthur and Elsie were chatting happily, catching up on the months they'd been apart, and Tilly was still buzzing with excitement after her

boating expedition. But Violet was unusually quiet –
even for her.

Eventually Tilly tried to draw her into the
conversation. 'Violet,' she said. 'Did you study much
maths while I was gone?'

Violet shook her head. 'No,' she said bitterly.
'What's the point? What's the point of anything for
a cripple like me?'

'Hey,' I said. 'Don't talk like that. Things will be
different after the war. You just wait and see.'

Violet shook her head even more violently. 'No
they won't. Not for me. By the time this war is over
I'll be too old for school and I'll still be too poor
for university. My education is over forever. I'll
probably end up in an institution for useless
people.'

'That so isn't true,' said Tilly, but Violet just
turned away with tears in her eyes.

I lay back on the grass and tried to think of a way
to help. In my real life, I knew there were all kinds
of organizations whose only job was helping people
with disabilities, but maybe that wasn't going to

happen for decades – much too late for Violet.
Then I thought of something that might make
Violet feel good about herself.

'While you were away, Tilly, Violet and I spent a
lot of time at The Willows,' I said. 'And Violet did
crosswords. She is totally amazing. She can solve a
cryptic crossword in the time it takes me to brush
my teeth.'

'Wow,' said Tilly. 'I'm impressed. Those things
are impossible.'

Violet gave a big sigh. 'I know you're both trying
to make me feel better, and I appreciate that – but
this doesn't change anything. Solving cryptic
crosswords won't save our soldiers.'

I sat up so quickly I felt dizzy. 'Omigod,' I said. 'I
have just had the most amazing idea. Why didn't we
think of this before?'

'Think of what?' said Tilly, but I ignored her as I
stood up and raced over to where Arthur and Elsie
were sitting in the shade of a tree. Violet and Tilly
followed me.

'Arthur?' I said.

He looked up and smiled his twinkly smile. 'What can I do for you, young lady?'

'Well, you know your top-secret work in Bletchley Park – the top-secret work we're not allowed to talk about?'

'Yes,' he said, looking all around as if there might be a squadron of enemy soldiers hiding behind the hedge.

'Are civilians allowed to help?'

He nodded. 'Of course they are. This work is very specialized, and we need all the best people we can get.'

'Well, if, say, we knew someone who is amazing at maths and all kinds of puzzles, and can solve cryptic crosswords in a few minutes, would they be useful?'

'Of course they would. That sounds like exactly the kind of person we're looking for.'

'Yessss!' I said. 'Arthur, meet Violet. She's just the person you need.'

He looked at her doubtfully. She was pale and skinny and young-looking, and she was balancing on her crutch and looking totally awkward.

'I don't really think –' began Arthur, but I stopped him.

'She'll prove it to you. Won't you, Violet?'

'I don't really think –' she began, but I stopped her too.

'Are there any newspapers around?' I asked Elsie.

She thought for a moment. 'Just the one that was wrapped round the fish I bought yesterday. It's still in the kitchen, I think.'

I raced inside and came back with the crumpled fishy paper and a pencil. 'Go on,' I said, holding them towards Violet. 'Show Arthur what you can do.'

Now Violet looked totally embarrassed, but Arthur nodded at her encouragingly. She sat down on the grass and I found the crossword page, flattened out the paper as well as I could and handed it to her. Then she took the pencil, chewed it once, and set to work. The rest of us watched with interest, and I noticed Arthur slyly glancing at his watch.

Violet worked steadily, sometimes sighing, and

177

sometimes smiling happily. Finally she put her pencil down. 'All done,' she said.

Arthur looked at his watch. 'Nine and a half minutes,' he said.

'Is that good?' asked Tilly.

'Yes,' he said. 'I have to say, that is very, very good. Exceptional even.'

Then he took the crossword and examined it. 'Not a single mistake, as far as I can see. That's really quite astonishing.'

Violet beamed.

'Tell me,' asked Arthur. 'Have you any knowledge of algebra?'

That sounded like a tricky question to me, but Violet looked at him like he'd asked her if she knew how to count up to five.

'I've been studying algebra for three years,' she said.

By now Arthur was looking very, very happy.

Elsie joined the conversation. 'I don't like to rain on your parade,' she said, 'but don't you think that maybe Violet is a bit young for this sort of thing?

She's just a girl. When I was her age I was still at home playing with kittens.'

Arthur nodded. 'You're absolutely right, Mother,' he said. 'Under normal circumstances, Violet *would be* a bit young, but there's a war on, and in a war, exceptions have to be made.'

'So she's in?' I asked, impatient for everything to be sorted.

Arthur smiled. 'I'll need to bring her for an interview with some of my supervisors, but it's looking like Violet's skills could be very useful indeed.'

Violet still looked uncertain. 'Me? Me do something useful?' she asked.

Tilly grinned. 'Yes. Now you and Arthur need to have a nice geeky maths talk. Don't worry about Lauren and me – we'll just sit here and chat with Elsie.'

'It will be so very nice for Violet to feel useful at last,' said Elsie as we sat down beside her.

'Totally,' I said. 'But what about you, Elsie? You're doing a great job here, taking care of Tilly and Violet and me, but after the war, what are you going to do?'

Elsie laughed. 'The same as I did before the war, I suppose.'

'And that was?' asked Tilly.

'Nothing very much. My most important job was being a good wife to Percy and a good mother to Arthur. I did both of those things as best I could, but now that those jobs are done I suppose there's nothing left for me.'

'That so isn't fair,' said Tilly.

'You'll be totally bored, just sitting here doing nothing,' I said.

Elsie nodded. 'You're probably right, but luckily I was raised without many expectations.'

'Everyone needs a purpose in life,' said Tilly. 'We're not going to let you rot here, doing nothing, Elsie. Now think, Lauren – we've sorted out Violet's career, so what do you suggest for Elsie?'

'Cooking?' I suggested. 'You're a total genius at making nice meals out of whatever weird ingredients the shop happens to have in stock. You make amazing cakes out of only scraps of butter and sugar, and your dinners are the best I've had in decades.'

Elsie smiled. 'Why thank you, my dear,' she said. 'But I very much hope that this war will end soon, and when it does, no one will want to just make do. My skills will be completely out of date.'

'There has to be something else,' said Tilly. 'There just has to be.'

'Omigod,' I said. 'I have it. I have the perfect post-war career for Elsie.'

'And it is?' asked Tilly.

'She should be a writer.'

Elsie laughed out loud. 'Me a writer? I don't think so. I'm barely educated.'

I ignored her protest. Now that the idea was sinking in, I was beginning to get very enthusiastic. 'You'd be perfect. Those stories you tell us about life in India when you were a little girl are amazing. Sometimes I think I'm going to die laughing when you describe the tricks you used to play on the servants.'

'And the drawings you did on our Christmas presents,' said Tilly, joining in, 'they were totally gorgeous. So you could write the books and illustrate them too. You could make a whole series. You could be rich and famous.'

'I'm not sure that I want to be rich and famous,' said Elsie, but she was smiling, and I could see that she was warming to the idea.

'Start with the story about the kittens you rescued,' said Tilly. 'Little kids would really, really love to hear that one. And then you could . . .'

She went on to list all of our favourite stories, and as she did so, Elsie's smile began to get bigger and brighter, and I knew that she was totally hooked.

'And I have the perfect title for the series,' I said. 'Elsie in India.'

Elsie clapped her hands together like a little girl, and then seemed embarrassed by her exuberance. 'I'll think about it,' she said primly.

'Sorted,' said Tilly. 'Now I'll get a pen and paper and you can get started on the first one.'

*

When George arrived half an hour later, we were still sitting in the garden. He joined us and we all sat there together, enjoying the relaxing morning.

Violet was beginning to panic about her big break. 'What on earth will I wear for my interview at Bletchley Park?' she wailed. 'Even if I had money to buy a dress, there aren't any in the local shop. All they've got is farm wear.'

Elsie put aside her writing and patted her on the arm. 'Make do and mend,' she said. 'It's my specialty. Now, you have that lovely purple velvet dress one of the neighbours gave you, and I've been saving some pearl buttons from a shirt of mine that wore out. The buttons will brighten up the dress beautifully, and you'll look like a little princess.'

'Thank you so very much,' said Violet. 'All this is like a dream come true.'

I lay on the grass, stroking Tiddles and feeling very pleased with myself. The sun was shining, my stomach was full of pancakes and my friends were happy. Then, just when I was thinking that things couldn't get any better, Tiddles arched his back and began to hiss. Tilly jumped to her feet and gasped.

'Omigod,' she said. 'Saturn's back.'

 20

Saturn was strolling casually along the garden wall, like he'd just wandered off for a few minutes. He didn't look thin or dirty or anything. I wondered where he'd been, and who had been taking care of him.

I raced over, picked him up and hugged him tight. Then I handed him to Tilly, and she did the same.

'Where have you been?' I asked as I stroked my pet. 'It's been months and months and months. I thought Tilly and I were going to be –' I stopped when I saw the others staring at me and corrected myself. 'I mean, I missed you a lot, and you will never, never know how happy I am to see you.'

Everyone else came over and said how glad they were that Saturn was back, and as they stroked and petted him, Saturn seemed to smile, like he was very pleased with himself.

'Come on,' said Tilly after a while. 'Let's take you inside.'

I followed them into the house and up to our bedroom. 'There is no way I'm letting you escape again, Saturn,' I said. I closed the door carefully behind us and checked that the window was firmly latched shut, forgetting for a minute that locked doors and windows were never going to be much of an obstacle to a cat who could travel through time.

Tilly and I sat down on the bed, and we beamed at each other.

'He's back,' I sighed. 'I can't believe he's back. I'd really given up hope.'

'It's like he was hiding somewhere, waiting for us to sort everyone out,' said Tilly.

'What do you mean?'

'Well, George and I went to Dunkirk and rescued all those soldiers, and it's looking like Violet's going to be an amazing code-breaker, and Elsie's going to be a famous writer. Like I said, we've sorted everyone out.'

I knew she was right.

'So it's time for us to leave?' I asked. 'I so badly want to see my family again. It feels like years and years since we left home.'

'I just want to give my dad the biggest hug ever,' she said. 'And, besides, this war's going to get a whole lot worse before it gets better.'

I picked Saturn up and held him tight. 'And there's another thing too. We can't take any chances with this guy. I'm not giving him the opportunity to go off without us again.'

Tilly and I looked at each other for a minute, wondering what to do next. 'Everyone's been so nice to us for all these months,' she said in the end. 'We can't just disappear without saying goodbye, can we?'

'But we can't exactly tell the truth either. How can we say: *It's been nice, but Tilly and I really belong to the twenty-first century, and we need to get back home before our dinner gets cold?*'

187

Tilly giggled. 'Too far, I think. Let's just go down and kind of half say goodbye.'

I'm not sure how exactly you half say goodbye, but, still, I carefully locked Saturn into the bedroom and followed Tilly downstairs and out to the garden where Elsie was still chatting to Arthur and George.

We both went over and hugged Elsie.

'It's always nice to be hugged,' said Elsie when we let her go. 'But is there a special reason for this?'

'Well, you've been really kind to us while we've been here,' I said.

'And we've been very happy with you,' said Tilly.

'Even though we've missed our families,' I added. As I said the words, I felt how true they were. I was looking forward to seeing my family in a way I'd never have thought possible – it was almost like a real, physical pain.

'And your families must be missing you,' said Elsie.

'Oh well,' said Tilly vaguely. 'They are and they aren't. But, either way, Lauren and I kind of think we'll have to go home soon.'

I had a sudden flash of inspiration. 'And, like when Tilly had to rush home to see her grandmother the other day, it might all happen very quickly. There might not be time to say goodbye.'

'And if we have to leave in a hurry, we'd feel really bad if we hadn't thanked you properly,' said Tilly.

Everyone was now looking a bit puzzled at our weird behaviour, but Tilly and I managed to ignore this as we turned to Arthur. 'Thanks for promising to bring Violet to Bletchley Park,' I said to him. 'I think working with you will change her life.'

'Violet is the one who will be helping us,' he said. 'That girl has potential to be one of our best workers.'

I now turned to George. I desperately wanted to hug him, but didn't dare. 'If the war is still on when you're old enough to sign up,' I said as I shook his hand formally, 'and if you do sign up . . . be careful. You need to come home safely. Violet will be waiting for you.'

At this, Tilly giggled, and George's face went redder than I had ever before seen it.

'I don't know what all these goodbyes are about,' he said gruffly. 'You two will feel proper stupid tomorrow when we're all still here together.'

These people were amazingly nice and kind, but, even so, I very much wished that my next tomorrow was going to be at home with my real family in my real life.

Tilly and I walked back to the house. 'Just in case,' I said. 'Goodbye, everyone!'

'Laters,' said Tilly.

Then we opened the door and went inside.

We found Violet in the kitchen, already sewing the first of Elsie's pearl buttons on to her dress. Just then, one of the buttons slipped from her fingers and fell to the floor. 'Oh fiddlesticks!' she said, making me smile.

I picked up the button. It was small and dainty and just perfect. I rolled it between my fingers, enjoying the cool smoothness of it. 'It's absolutely beautiful,' I said.

Violet smiled. 'You can have it if you like – there's one spare. You could sew it on to one of your dresses.'

I thought of the ugly dresses that I'd almost got used to wearing over the past months. 'Thanks,' I said. 'But I won't sew it on to my dress. I've got a much better idea. I'm going to put it on my bracelet.'

I took off my charm bracelet and clipped the pearl button into a space. Then I lay the bracelet on the table. Violet touched the charms one by one.

'They are so gorgeous,' she said.

'Thanks,' I said. 'Some of them are very special to me – like this medal, and the little Roman girl. I got them from friends who . . . well . . . friends who I don't see any more.'

Violet was looking at the ship charm. 'That's the *Titanic*,' she said. 'I never noticed that before. It sank, you know.'

Tilly and I grinned at each other. 'Lauren knows better than you'd think,' said Tilly. 'She knows so much it's almost like she was there.'

'Anyway, Violet,' I said. 'I'd like to give you one of my charms – in exchange for the pearl button.'

'But I couldn't,' said Violet. 'How could I take

one of your special charms in exchange for just a button?'

'It's more than a button to me,' I said. 'It's a present from a friend.'

Then I noticed that Violet was paying extra attention to the small pink cupcake charm. I quickly unclipped it.

'Here,' I said. 'You can put it in your pocket, and it will bring you luck at your Bletchley Park interview.'

Violet thanked me, and we were all quiet for a minute.

Violet had become a great friend, and yet this huge lie was hanging between us. How could Tilly and I just go upstairs and disappear from Violet's life forever?

And yet, even if we tried to explain the truth, how could Violet possibly believe what we were saying?

How could anything so bizarre be true?

So Tilly and I both hugged Violet, and hoped that would be enough.

'Friends forever?' I whispered.

'Forever and a day,' said Violet, and then I pulled away and ran upstairs before she could see my tears.

Tilly and I pulled our own clothes from a box under the bed, and changed back into them. We sat on the bed, and Saturn jumped into my arms, like he knew what was going on.

'Be sure to touch him at all times,' I said to Tilly. 'I really don't want to leave you behind.'

'And I really, really don't want to be left behind,' said Tilly, giggling nervously.

'Come on,' I said to Saturn as I started to stroke him. 'We've been waiting months and months for this, so let's not make a mess of it. Just concentrate, and bring us back home, OK?'

Saturn blinked once, then opened his blue and green eyes wide, like he understood what I was saying.

I looked at the matching blue and green stones on his collar. 'I have no idea how this works,' I said. 'So how about you press a blue stone, Tilly, and I'll press a green one, and we'll see what happens?'

Tilly nodded. Then she began to whisper over and over: 'There's no place like home. There's no place like home.'

'Now,' I said, and together we pressed the stones. At first nothing happened and then the familiar bright white light washed over us, and a deafening noise started in our ears, and a second later . . .

'We're home!' laughed Tilly. 'We're really and truly home!'

21

'Omigod,' I sighed. 'That was the most amazing mystery tour ever.'

My heart was thumping madly as I looked around my bedroom. I felt the unbelievably soft cushions on my bed, and looked at my half-open wardrobe, which was stuffed with gorgeous, modern clothes.

'Thanks, Saturn,' I said, and then I put him on the floor and raced downstairs, with Tilly following close behind me.

Mum was still in the hall. 'Did you hear that, Lauren?' she asked. 'Honestly, your sister will drive me to . . . well, I'm not sure what she'll drive me to, but –'

She didn't get a chance to finish as I threw myself into her arms. 'Oh, Mum,' I blurted out. 'I love you so much, and I've missed you so much, and . . .'

Just then Amy came charging back in. 'Ha, Lauren,' she said, 'just because I'm in trouble, you're trying to suck up to Mum. We can all see through you, you know.'

I grinned at her. I didn't care that she was angry, and that she was picking on me. All I cared was that I was home again.

I let go of Mum and hugged Amy.

'Weirdo,' she muttered, pushing me away. 'Total loser weirdo.'

'Poor Lauren,' said Mum, putting her arm round me. 'You're always getting caught in the crossfire.'

Tilly giggled. 'I've seen real crossfire, Deirdre, and, trust me, what goes on in your house is nothing compared to that.'

Mum laughed, even though she couldn't have had the faintest idea what Tilly was on about.

She led me into the kitchen. 'Come on, girls,' she said. 'Tea won't be ready for a while, so why don't you get yourselves a snack?'

Tilly followed us into the kitchen, and we both gasped. Tilly ran over to the fruit bowl, and looked like she was going to drool all over it. She picked up an orange and rolled it around in her hands. She smelled it and gazed at it like it was the most wonderful thing she had ever seen. For a horrible moment, I thought she was going to kiss it. Hoping to distract her, I opened the fridge, and what I saw there took my breath away.

'So much food!' I gasped.

Mum pretended to slap me on the leg. 'Don't be sarcastic, miss,' she said. 'I haven't had time to go shopping for the last few days.'

'I wasn't being sarcastic,' I said. But how could I hope to explain?

How could I find words to describe how wonderful a shelf half full of yoghurt and cheese and ham looked?

How could I look at a cupboard stacked with

sugar and flour, and not wonder how many ration books would be needed to buy such amounts?

And so I said nothing as I made a fat, juicy and delicious sandwich for myself and my friend.

As soon as Tilly finished eating, she got ready to go home.

'You can stay for tea if you like,' said Mum.

Tilly shook her head. 'Thanks, but no thanks, Deirdre,' she said. 'I need to get home. It feels like a lifetime since I saw my dad.'

'That's so sweet of you,' said Mum, and Tilly just laughed and skipped off home.

When I woke next morning I lay for a while with my eyes closed, and tried to plan my day. If it was sunny, maybe Tilly and Violet and I could go for a swim. And after lunch, George might take us to pick elderflowers so Elsie could make lemonade with next week's sugar rations.

'Hey, Till–' I began, but she wasn't curled up asleep next to me. Then sounds began to work their way into my head. I could hear Amy's hairdryer and the sound of Dad and Stephen loudly discussing football.

I opened my eyes, and looked around my own bedroom, which suddenly seemed strange and unfamiliar.

How could real life seem so . . . unreal?

After what felt like a huge breakfast of cereal and toast and orange juice, I went over to Tilly's place.

'How do you feel?' she asked as we settled down on her bed.

'Weird. You?'

'Totally weird.'

'And what did your dad say when you told him about your phone?' I asked.

'Well, I couldn't tell him the truth, could I? He'd hardly believe me if I said that I lost it during an air raid in 1939, would he?'

I laughed. 'So what did you tell him?'

'I was kind of vague,' she said. 'But he was reading the newspaper at the time, so he wasn't paying much attention anyway.'

'Always a good plan,' I said. 'Anyway, are we ready to do a bit of Googling? Are you ready to find out what happened to all our old friends?'

She hesitated. 'I'm not sure. There was a war on, remember.'

'I noticed,' I said.

'And things might not have turned out very well for them.'

'But don't you really want to know?'

She nodded. 'Yeah, I really, really want to know. Wait there and I'll get the laptop.'

Minutes later, Tilly had typed in *Violet Rudford* and the cursor was poised over the search button. I nodded and she clicked. A second later three words flashed up on the screen:

NO RESULTS FOUND.

'Weird,' I said.

'Totally. Let's try Elsie.'

But there was no result for Elsie either, or for George.

'I can't believe it,' I sighed. 'We knew these people. We lived with them for months. How come there's not a single mention of any of them on the Internet? It's like they never existed.'

Tilly shrugged. 'Maybe we shouldn't be surprised. It's not like they were going to show up on Facebook or Twitter, is it? I suppose only people who were famous in 1940 are going to show up on the Internet after all these years.'

'But when we left them they had such great plans. What could have happened to Elsie's books? And Violet's code-breaking?'

'Maybe none of that stuff worked out – and maybe that doesn't matter. My dad's always saying that people nowadays are obsessed with fame. Maybe the ordinary lives Elsie and Violet lived while we were there just went on and on. Maybe they lived happily ever after – in a quiet, non-famous kind of way.'

I didn't want to believe her. I didn't want it to end just like this.

'Try Bletchley Park,' I said.

Tilly did as I asked, and pages and pages of information showed up. We even found a photograph of all the code-breakers, but it was fuzzy and distant, and even though we tried for ages, we couldn't make out any faces. We couldn't find Arthur or Violet.

I still didn't want to give up. 'Try –' I began, but I was interrupted by Tilly's dad calling up the stairs. 'Tilly, it's a beautiful day,' he said. 'Turn off that computer and go out and get some fresh air. You've been indoors all week.'

'Actually,' muttered Tilly to me, 'I've been living a very healthy outdoors life recently, and this is the first time I've touched a computer in more than nine months.' But, still, she did as she was told and we went outside. Tilly started to walk purposefully towards town.

'You look like you've got a plan,' I said as I hurried after her.

She grinned. 'Of course I've got a plan. Remember, Lauren, the Internet is a useful tool, but it's not infallible.'

Soon we were at the local bookshop and I followed Tilly up to the Customer Service desk.

'We're looking for a book by Elsie Chilcott,' she said.

The woman keyed the name into the computer, and then shook her head. 'Sorry. There's nothing showing up.'

'But there has to be,' I protested.

The woman gave me a funny look. 'I can assure you there's nothing there.'

I felt really, really disappointed and it must have shown on my face, as the woman smiled. 'Maybe the book you're looking for is out of print,' she said. 'And sometimes out-of-print books don't show up on my system.'

'Or maybe it was never actually published at all,' muttered Tilly under her breath.

'What is the book about?' asked the woman.

'It would be a children's book,' I said. 'It should be lots of stories about a little girl called Elsie who lived in —'

Before I could finish, Tilly and the shop assistant

spoke together. '*Elsie in India*,' they said, and we all laughed.

The girl typed on her computer again. '*Elsie in India*. I'm afraid it *is* out of print. And you had the wrong author name – it was written by a woman called Elsie Ellingham.'

Tilly giggled. 'Elsie used a pen-name. Who'd have guessed?'

'And that's why we couldn't find her on the Internet,' I said.

'I've never even seen that book,' said the shop assistant. 'But my mother used to talk about it all the time. It was *her* mother's favourite book when she was a little girl.'

'So do you know where we could get a copy?'

The woman thought for a moment. 'Well, since it's out of print, I can't get it for you. You could keep an eye on the second-hand sites on the Internet – or it might be worth having a look in the antique bookshop on Market Street.'

We thanked her and raced off to Market Street. We soon found the bookshop and walked in, blinking in the darkness. Stacks of old and dusty books covered every surface.

'No e-books here, I guess,' giggled Tilly.

'I'm glad it's not an e-book,' I said. 'I want to find Elsie's *real* book. I want to hold it in my hand and smell it and turn the pages – the way she intended it to be used.'

An old man appeared out of the darkness. 'Well, young ladies, what can I do for you?' he asked.

We told him the name of the book we were looking for and he smiled. 'I read that book when I was just a boy,' he said. 'Very popular it was too – in the forties and fifties. There was a whole series of them, you know. Then that kind of thing went out of fashion. Stories about little girls and their servants aren't considered very politically correct these days. I sometimes think –'

'Er . . . the book?' I interrupted, trying not to sound too impatient. 'Do you think you might have a copy?'

The man smiled, his white teeth almost glowing

in the gloom. 'Do you know, I think I do. Let me just have a look back here.'

He vanished into a storeroom at the back of the shop, and there was lots of clattering and banging and sighing. Tilly and I exchanged nervous glances. Finally, the man reappeared, rubbing the dust off a tattered old book.

'I knew it was in there somewhere,' he said, handing it to Tilly.

'Omigod,' I said. 'I can't believe this. How much is it?'

I was suddenly afraid that an antique like this would cost thousands of Euro, but the man just smiled. 'It's been gathering dust back there for the best part of twenty years. If you promise to give it a good home, I think I can let you have it for nothing.'

'Thanks!' Tilly and I said together, and we raced off to read our book.

We sat on a wall outside and gazed at our treasure. Tilly opened the first page and gasped.

'What?' I asked, leaning across her to look.

And then I saw the dedication.

To my wartime girls – Violet, Lauren and Tilly.
Without you, this never would have happened.

'Omigod,' I said. 'How cool is that?'

'Totally,' said Tilly. 'We were famous before we were born. Whoever would have guessed that?'

And we both laughed.

22

We spent a long time reading Elsie's book, and admiring her beautiful watercolour illustrations. When I got to the story about the stray kittens, it was almost like Elsie was sitting right beside me, whispering in my ear. It was totally weird, but nice too.

We were walking back to her place when Tilly grabbed me. 'We are totally, totally stupid,' she said.

'Speak for yourself,' I muttered.

'OK,' she said, laughing. 'But you'll agree when I tell you what I've just thought of. Maybe Violet Rudford didn't exist after the war.'

'But what could have happened to her? She should

have been safe in the country with Elsie. How could she . . .?'

Tilly giggled. 'That's not what I meant. What I meant was, what if her surname wasn't Rudford any more?'

At last I understood. 'You mean she might have got married?'

Tilly nodded. 'Exactly. And it wasn't the twenty-first century, so if she got married, she'd definitely have changed her name.'

Now I was getting excited too. 'Maybe she married George,' I said. 'How totally romantic would that be?'

'And not just romantic,' added Tilly. 'It might mean that we can find out what happened to her during and after the war.'

'Omigod,' I said. 'You're right.'

We hurried the last bit to Tilly's house and ran up to her bedroom and switched on her laptop. With shaking hands, I typed two words: *Violet Dykins.*

This time there were lots of results.

'It looks like there are two people called Violet

Dykins,' said Tilly. 'And I don't believe it – one of them is on Facebook.'

We found the Facebook Violet, and then collapsed laughing, as the picture of a smiley-faced black woman from Chicago popped up.

'I know it's been a while,' I said. 'But I don't think she could have changed all that much.'

'Let's try the other one,' said Tilly, wiping away her tears of laughter.

There was only one result for the other Violet, leading us to an article in a small English local newspaper. This time there was no picture, but I felt like jumping up and down when I read the article's title –

LOCAL WOMAN WAS WARTIME
CODE-BREAKING HERO

We read the article to the end, and then I sat back on Tilly's bed and sighed. 'It's so cool. That has to be our Violet – and it means she married George.'

'And it means she *did* go on to be a code-breaker.

And did you see where it said she went to university after the war and became a maths professor? That's a great result for someone who said she'd never be any use to anyone.'

'And it means something else,' I said. 'It means that Violet is still alive – or she was three months ago when she gave the interview for that article.'

'Wow,' said Tilly. 'That is so totally weird. When you came back from 1914, all the people you had met were dead, and it was the same when we both went to Pompeii – Prima died thousands of years before we were born.'

'But Violet is alive,' I said. 'We could meet her. We could talk to her. We could . . .'

But Tilly wasn't listening to me any more. She was busy on the laptop, and as soon as she finished she picked up her phone.

'What are you doing?' I asked, afraid that I already knew the answer.

'Luckily Dykins is a really unusual name. There's only one Violet Dykins in the whole of the English phone book.'

'And I'm guessing you're planning to call that number?'

She nodded.

'And what are you going to say?'

She sighed. 'I don't really know – yet. But don't you think it would be totally cool to talk to Violet again?'

'Of course it would. But we have to be careful. Violet must be in her eighties by now. Don't say anything that could give her a shock. She might have a heart attack or something.'

Tilly rolled her eyes and started to key in the number. Then she switched her phone's speaker on and I tried not to shake with excitement as the harsh ringing sound filled the room. Then there was a click, and a voice. 'Hello?'

Tilly took a deep breath. 'I'd like to speak to Violet Dykins, please.'

'This is Violet speaking.'

Tilly looked at me, asking a silent question. I shrugged. This was an old person's voice, so how was I supposed to know if it belonged to the girl who was once our friend?

'Er . . . my name is Tilly,' said Tilly. 'And my friend Lauren is here with me too.'

'And how can I help you?'

I put my head down, unable to hide my disappointment. The woman didn't recognize our names. Either it was the wrong woman, or she had forgotten us completely.

I tried to mime hanging up to Tilly, but she ignored me.

'We'd like to talk to you about a project we're doing at school.'

Now the woman laughed, but it was a kind, gentle laugh. 'I don't know what possible use to your project I could be.'

'It's . . . it's about your experiences . . . in the war . . . you know . . . code-breaking and stuff.'

The woman laughed again. 'You've got the wrong woman,' she said. 'I was born long after the war ended. It's my mother you're looking for – she's called Violet too.'

Tilly grinned at me. 'Yes,' she said. 'I guess it is. We saw the article in the paper, and it was really interesting. Do you think your mother would help us?'

'I'm quite sure she would. For many years, she refused to talk about how she spent the war, but lately she's changed completely. She wants to tell her story. I think she's afraid that young people will forget how dreadful the war really was.'

'So could we speak to her, please?'

'I'm so sorry. My mother doesn't live around here any more. She wasn't managing very well on her own, so she's gone to live with my sister. I can give you my sister's phone number if you like?'

'That would be great,' said Tilly.

'Only the call will be expensive for you,' she said. 'Since my sister lives in Ireland.'

Now Tilly was nearly jumping up and down with excitement. 'But so do we,' she said. 'Do you think your mother would agree to meet us? That would be so totally cool and amazing.'

The woman laughed one more time. 'I think that's very possible,' she said. 'Now have you got a pen? I'll give you the number.'

23

A few days later, Tilly and I were pulling out of the city in her dad's car.

'You young ones,' he said, pretending to be cross. 'In my day, research for a project meant a few hours in the local library, not persuading your poor long-suffering dad to drive you halfway across the country to conduct an interview with some little old lady.'

Tilly just laughed. 'You're helping my education, Dad,' she said. 'Now drive faster, we don't want to be late.'

Forty minutes later, we were standing outside a pretty thatched cottage.

'I'll be back in an hour,' said Tilly's dad. 'But I expect you'll be finished in ten minutes. The poor old woman will have probably told you her entire life story by then.'

Tilly giggled. 'You'd be surprised, Dad. Now off you go and let us get started.'

'This is going to be totally weird,' I said as we walked up the short path. 'Violet hasn't seen us for more than seventy years, and yet we haven't changed in the slightest.'

'And we saw her last week, but in those few days she's managed to change from a young girl to . . . well, we'll see what she's changed to in a few minutes.'

A friendly woman answered the door and led us out to the garden at the back of the cottage. She pointed to where an old grey-haired lady was dozing on a wicker chair, next to a small table.

'Mother,' she called. 'Here are the two girls who want to talk to you. Remember I told you they'd be calling over this afternoon?'

Just then the phone inside the house rang. 'Please

216

excuse me,' said the woman. 'I need to answer that. I'll be inside if you need me.'

Then she walked away, leaving Tilly and me alone with our dear old friend. This should have been a totally happy and exciting moment – but it wasn't. I was totally terrified, and part of me wanted to turn round and race after Tilly's dad and beg him to take us straight back home again.

Long minutes passed, but neither Tilly nor I moved. In our heads we knew that Violet had to be in her eighties, but even so . . .

Finally, Tilly started to walk towards the woman, and I followed, one step behind. As we drew close, the woman opened her eyes, and looked at us. I gulped. Violet's eyes had been a clear, beautiful green, but the eyes gazing at me were dull and red-rimmed, and half covered by saggy old flesh. Violet was supposed to have perfect pale freckled skin, but the face in front of us was greyish, and deeply lined. The once thick and shiny red hair was dull and grey and wispy.

I had a sudden vision of the day Violet first swam

in the sea. I could see her flinging her arms out with joy. I could see her sparkling eyes, and her beautiful red hair flying in the wind.

'I'm not sure . . .' I began to whisper to Tilly, but now the woman was pulling herself slowly off her chair, getting ready to greet us.

This was just too weird, and I very much wished that I was somewhere, anywhere else.

Then the woman's arm nudged against the table, and the crutch that was resting against it fell to the ground.

'Oh fiddlesticks!' she said, and shook her head quickly from side to side.

All at once, it was as if the years had slipped away.

'Violet!' said Tilly and I together, and we ran over and hugged our friend.

When we finally let go, Violet sat down heavily on her chair. 'My, my,' she said, smiling. 'I wasn't expecting that nice warm greeting – but at my age, every hug is precious so I'm not complaining. Now, my daughter tells me that you two girls are working on a history project, and that you want to interview me.'

And then, I couldn't hold back any more. 'Violet,' I said. 'It's me, Lauren. And this is Tilly. We were friends – a long time ago. Don't you remember us?'

Now Violet reached for the glasses that were hanging round her neck. With a shaking hand, she put them on. She gazed at us for a long time, and then she took off the glasses, polished them with the corner of her cardigan and put them on again.

'Lauren? Tilly?' she said faintly.

We smiled at her.

'Yes,' I said. 'I know it's totally weird and impossible, but it really is us.'

Violet looked at Tilly for a long time and then she turned her gaze on me. She put her hand to her own old, wrinkled face.

'That can't be right,' she said faintly. 'You're both so . . . young.'

She leaned forward, and her collar slipped to one side. I could see a thin chain round her neck, and on it there hung a small charm. It wasn't shiny and pink any more. It was chipped and worn – but there was no mistaking my cupcake charm.

I gasped, and held my charm bracelet towards Violet, showing her the small pearl button she'd given me days, or decades, before.

Violet reached out and touched it with a thin, mottled finger.

'Elsie's button,' she whispered. 'Like the ones she gave me for my velvet dress. It's really you . . . and yet . . .?'

Tilly and I sat down on the grass beside her chair. 'It's totally, totally complicated,' Tilly said. 'And even if we could explain, it would take ages and ages, and . . .'

'And we can only stay an hour,' I finished for her. 'So do you think you could survive without explanations and just talk to us instead?'

Violet smiled, and for one fleeting second, I could see the girl we had once known.

'The older I get,' she said, 'the less I believe in explanations. Most things are not at all as simple as they seem. And, besides, even though I liked you two girls very much, I always suspected that there was something very strange and unpredictable about you both.'

Now I felt embarrassed. I'd thought that Tilly and I had done a good job of blending into 1940, but maybe people had just been too polite to point out that they thought we were a bit weird.

But Violet was smiling. 'So let's go for it,' she said. 'As you young people say nowadays. What would you like to talk about?'

Tilly and I looked at each other. There were so many questions we could ask, and it was hard to know exactly where to start.

'We're not really doing a history project,' said Tilly in the end. 'We just wanted to see you again. We'd like to know what happened next. After we left.'

Violet folded her arms, settled back in her chair, and began to speak. 'You left rather suddenly, didn't you?' she began. 'You'd been acting strangely that day, I remember.'

'Sorry about that,' I said, and then Violet continued.

'But even though I missed you . . . well . . . it was wartime, after all, and there was a lot of coming and going back then. We learned not to ask too many questions.'

'Just the way Arthur liked it,' giggled Tilly.

'Exactly,' continued Violet with a small smile. 'After you left, I met with Arthur's commanding officers, and then things happened very quickly indeed. I moved to Bletchley Park, or The Park, as we always called it. I spent the rest of the war there, working on code-breaking. Funny how you knew what was going on there, since it was all so very top secret.'

'Oh, well,' said Tilly airily. 'I've always been good at guessing stuff.'

'And did you like it at The Park?' I asked. 'Did you enjoy the work?'

Violet gave a big long sigh. 'I loved my time at The Park,' she said. 'The workers there were like one big happy family. Sometimes the work could be a bit tedious, but every now and then we made a big breakthrough, and the excitement of that was breathtaking. We really felt as if we were making a difference, as if we were saving lives.'

'And what happened after the war?' I asked. I didn't want to rush her, but I was afraid that Tilly's dad would be back before we'd had time to ask all our questions.

'After the war,' said Violet, 'I got the opportunity I'd always dreamed of. I went to university and studied mathematics. A wonderful career was stretching out in front of me, but . . .'

'But what?' I asked, afraid she was going to tell me that her disability had held her back again.

But a slow smile spread over Violet's face. 'But one weekend I went to visit Elsie and I bumped into George again. He'd spent many years in hospital. He lost a leg, you know – in 1945, just as the war was ending.'

'How awful,' said Tilly.

'Yes, it was awful,' said Violet. 'But at least he was

alive. And . . . well, if anyone understood how he felt, it had to be me.'

'That's so romantic,' sighed Tilly.

Violet smiled. 'It was perfect. A year later we married, and that was the end of my mathematics career.'

'After all your work,' I gasped. 'That seems so unfair.'

But Violet just laughed. 'That's the way things were back then. I didn't mind. All I wanted was the choice – the chance to prove that I could do something. And in the end I was satisfied with my choice. George and I were very happy together.'

'And is he still . . .?' I couldn't finish the question, and I was fairly sure I knew the answer anyway.

Violet shook her head. 'George passed away five years ago.'

'And your dad?' asked Tilly.

Violet gave a small sad smile. 'My father made it back from Dunkirk in 1940.'

'Maybe with George and me?' said Tilly.

'Maybe,' said Violet. 'With all the confusion of

224

that day, he never could say for sure. That didn't matter though. Some kind soul risked their life to save him.' She sat there for a minute, with a sad look on her face.

'And then?' I prompted.

'My father came and spent one wonderful week with me at Elsie's house that summer,' said Violet. 'It was a very special time for the two of us. He didn't survive the war though. He died in Greece in 1941.'

I didn't know what to say. How do you sympathize with a person about something that happened more than seventy years ago?

'It was sad,' said Violet. 'But it was wartime. Everyone lost loved ones. And in many ways, I was lucky. Elsie took care of me as well as if I were her own daughter.'

That reminded me. 'Elsie's book,' I said.

Violet laughed. 'Elsie turned out to be a bit of a celebrity for a while. She did many TV appearances in her later years. One of them I remember particularly well – it was in the seventies, I think.

She talked about you two girls and how you inspired her to write down her stories. But you probably saw that at the time?'

I shook my head, smiling. 'No. We might have been out of town when it was on.'

'So where did you and George live when you got married?' asked Tilly.

Violet smiled. 'We built a cottage right next to the sea – just like I'd always dreamed. The two of us swam every morning; I never forgot your swimming lessons, Tilly. George and I must have looked a strange pair, hopping into the water, but we didn't care. We were happy, the two of us, and we went on to have six lovely children. We lived a perfectly wonderful life – a life I'd never have dreamed of when I was a little girl growing up in London.'

'I'm so glad everything turned out well for you,' said Tilly, and I nodded in agreement.

After that, everything was fine. We chatted about Violet's life and her children, and about the book she was planning to write recalling her wartime experiences. And then, much, much too soon, we heard Tilly's dad's car pulling up outside the cottage.

We stood up and hugged Violet for a long time. Then Tilly and I reluctantly tore ourselves away and walked towards the garden gate. I had a horrible feeling that we would never see Violet again.

Violet's daughter came out of the house, and went over to Violet. Tilly and I stopped at the gate, and watched for a moment. 'They seemed like two nice girls,' we could hear the daughter saying. 'How did the interview go?'

'It went very well indeed,' said Violet. 'Talking to those two girls was like going right back in time. They were . . .' Then she stopped and shook her head. 'Oh fiddlesticks,' she said.

'What is it?' asked the daughter.

'I think the sunshine must have made me doze off,' said Violet. 'I had the most vivid dream about two girls I once knew. For a minute I almost believed that they were right here in the garden with me. It's amazing how real dreams can be.'

Tilly and I slipped through the gate and closed it

softly behind us. Then we heard Violet's next words. 'It was a lovely dream about two lovely girls who changed my life.'

Tilly and I hugged happily and then we climbed into her dad's car for the long journey home.

Bright and shiny and sizzling with fun stuff . . .

puffin.co.uk

WEB FUN

UNIQUE and exclusive digital content!
Podcasts, photos, Q&A, Day in the Life of, interviews and much more, from Eoin Colfer, Cathy Cassidy, Allan Ahlberg and Meg Rosoff to Lynley Dodd!

WEB NEWS

The **Puffin Blog** is packed with posts and photos from Puffin HQ and special guest bloggers. You can also sign up to our monthly newsletter **Puffin Beak Speak**

WEB CHAT

Discover something new EVERY month – books, competitions and treats galore

WEBBED FEET

(Puffins have funny little feet and brightly coloured beaks)

Point your mouse our way today!

It all started with a Scarecrow.

Puffin is seventy years old.
Sounds ancient, doesn't it? But Puffin has never been
so lively. We're always on the lookout for the next big
idea, which is how it began all those years ago.

Penguin Books was a big idea from the mind of
a man called Allen Lane, who in 1935 invented
the quality paperback and changed the world.
**And from great Penguins, great Puffins grew,
changing the face of children's books forever.**

The first four Puffin Picture Books were hatched in 1940 and the
first Puffin story book featured a man with broomstick arms called
Worzel Gummidge. In 1967 Kaye Webb, Puffin Editor, started the
Puffin Club, promising to **'make children into readers'**.
She kept that promise and over 200,000 children became
devoted Puffineers through their quarterly instalments of
Puffin Post, which is now back for a new generation.

Many years from now, we hope you'll look back and
remember Puffin with a smile. **No matter what your age
or what you're into, there's a Puffin for everyone.**
The possibilities are endless, but one thing is for sure:
whether it's a picture book or a paperback, a sticker book
or a hardback, **if it's got that little Puffin
on it – it's bound to be good.**